Leo Bruce's brilliantly ingenious new detective story opens with an extract from a diary: notes made by someone planning the 'perfect', the 'ideal' murder—the one which no police, no detective, could solve. The murderer's gratification will be entirely cerebral, his (or her) triumph being one of mind over matter.

Up to a point it would seem that nothing could be better planned: the place a remote shelter on the promenade at Selby-on-Sea, the occasion a blustery evening in late November, the victim almost ready-made for a crack of doom from a small coal-hammer. . . .

But this is not the first murderer whose plans are upset by an unexpected coincidence and in particular by the unpredictable mind of Carolus Deene, that unique schoolmaster-detective.

D1361955

SUCH IS DEATH

by

LEO BRUCE

Academy
Chicago
Publishers

Published in 1986 by

Academy Chicago Publishers
425 N. Michigan Avenue
Chicago, Illinois 60611

Copyright © 1963 by Propertius Company Ltd.

Printed and bound in the USA

No part of this book may be reproduced
in any form without the express written
permission of the publisher.

Library of Congress Cataloging-in-Publication Data

Bruce, Leo, 1903-1980.
    Such is death.

    I.   Title.
[PR6005.R673S83   1986]   823'.912   85-28737
ISBN 0-89733-159-1
ISBN 0-89733-160-5 (pbk.)

I

Extract from a Diary:

. . . T H E delicious sensation of being a murderer, a sensation given to few. I do not look for any physical satisfaction in this; I am no sadist, and the act in itself will be as repugnant to me as to anyone else. My gratification will be entirely cerebral, my triumph one of mind over matter.

That is one reason why I shall never be suspected. It is motive which gives the key to the identity of every murderer, even when his motive is no more than the satisfaction of some dark sexual desire to kill. The maniac who kills for the low perverted love of it can soon be identified, however normal his outward life may be. For one thing, he has to choose his victim; it is part of his paranoiac dream to kill this kind of person or that. My own complete indifference in this makes me immune from discovery. It can be man woman or child for all I care. I shall simply kill the first person who comes along.

That is the secret—to *have* no motive. When the body is found and enquiries begin, the first thing the investigators will ask themselves is—who had any reason to kill this person? And whoever the victim is, his or her circumstances will certainly provide a natural suspect. Even if it happens to be one of those dull people who ‘has not an enemy in the world’, who is neither envied nor hated, who stands in no one’s way and has never given offence, the investigators will ingeniously discover someone with a motive, or put the crime down to the aberration of a sex maniac. It will be inconceivable to them that a human being should have been killed with no motive at all. Or at least no motive which by the wildest flight of imagination could be perceived.

I do not want to kill, I want to have killed. I have no object in killing except to be able to say to myself that I have achieved it. So I shall never be found out.

This is the ideal town for my purpose. A small seaside resort in winter—what could be better? What I need is a lonely spot, but one to which a visit would cause no comment. I have it here. The promenade in the evening is lonely enough and any sound uttered is drowned by the noise of the sea. Yet no one would notice me walking along there. What could be more natural than a wish to take a breath of fresh air before turning in? Every evening a few people go out for their 'blow' after dinner. Not enough to threaten the solitude of the farthest shelter, for instance, but enough to make me inconspicuous as I walk away from the body.

Even if I were seen and recognized—highly unlikely—it would not begin to throw the least suspicion on me. Even I were caught red-handed, as it were, or at least found in the shelter with the corpse by someone who had come up too quickly to let me get away, I would only have to say I had just found it there. There would be absolutely nothing to connect me with the act. Someone has to find every corpse and it does not mean that the finder is ever suspected.

In fact, that seems rather a good idea. When I have got it over and the creature is dead, why don't I report the discovery? I shall have to think about this and make up my mind when I am considering the whole thing in more detail.

Yes, that last shelter is the place. It must be two hundred yards from the nearest houses for along there the road turns away from the sea and a small public garden (locked at night) lies between it and the promenade. There is enough light but not too much.

The beauty of it is that I am not tied to any particular time. I can wait till one night all the circumstances combine for my purpose. I need one person alone there and no one else in sight. I need a darkish windy night with a noisy sea, yet not really bad weather, for that would

6

make my presence on the promenade too remarkable. When I have these I shall do what I have decided to do—but not until then. If it does not come this year I shall wait till next—there is no hurry. But when it comes, no power on earth will be able to implicate me. I throw that out as a challenge to fate. We are always hearing of the perfect crime and the fatal mistake by which the murderer commits himself, or the coincidence or bad luck which gives him away. Here those things simply cannot exist. I can make no fatal slip because there is none to make, because no elaborate plans are necessary, because all I have to do is take my evening stroll and in the course of it do this one swift almost casual thing. There can be no coincidence or bad luck. If a policeman popped up out of nowhere, as you might say, I should only have to tell him that I had found a corpse in the shelter. With no motive I am entirely and certainly secure from consequences.

There is one other thing by which murderers have sometimes been identified, the method they choose or the implement they employ. I have been extremely cautious in planning this. The method must be one which does not by itself reveal the kind of person using it. It must be possible for everyone from a powerful man to a weak woman. And it must be certain and easily carried out against any sort of victim. It must also be instantaneous. Shooting is out, not only on account of the noise but because it would at once tell the investigator something, at least, about the murderer. Strangling could be very difficult if the victim resisted. Poisoning would be too slow and anyway my victim might refuse the chocolates I had prepared. Other methods involve implements by which the murderer could be identified—a swordstick, for instance. But I have it. An ordinary well-used very heavy hammer such as may be used for anything from breaking coal to driving in a stake. Such a one I have kept by me for years. No one knows I have it. It is small enough to carry with me unnoticeably and large enough to be effective.

So I shall take it with me—having cleaned it of finger-prints, of course, and not omitting to wear gloves—until the evening on which, as I say, the circumstances combine. One blow on the cranium can be given with it without any warning at all to anyone sitting in the shelter, and afterwards I leave it there. It is of everyday design and has been used for many purposes over the years. It cannot be identified for there are thousands like it in use in thousands of homes. The only thing the investigator might do is to look for some home from which such a hammer is missing. Let him find that: it will start him on yet another false trail.

It has an additional advantage. A murder committed with a tool which no one could be carrying by chance will look like a planned murder. Someone, the investigator will argue, was determined to kill this person and having armed himself or herself with a weapon for the purpose followed the victim to this shelter and carried out a carefully laid plan. That is exactly what I want him to think. It could not occur to him that such a plan might be made with no particular victim in mind and the investigator will at once start looking for some one with a motive for killing this particular person. If he was strangled with his own scarf, for instance, it could be an unpremeditated affair, perhaps for robbery.

That's another point. Shall I rob the corpse? It might suggest a motive particularly if the victim happens to be carrying anything valuable. I think on the whole no, for I do not believe a single human being lives without enemies or those who would find his death convenient. But I may decide to do it. It is another point I must consider, however.

Instinct tells me to do nothing to complicate the beautifully simple thing as it is by trying to supply false motives, or false anything else. I have always believed that if anyone walks out and kills the first person he sees for no reason at all he cannot be discovered unless he is actually caught in the act. But if he plans it too closely his conduct in anticipation of the event may give him away.

8

He builds up an alibi which fails in some detail or other, or by deliberately dissociating himself from the thing he makes some move, or passes some remark, which in the searchlights of investigation will show up. I shall do absolutely nothing that I do not ordinarily do and say nothing that I might not say at any time.

Nor do I want anyone else to share my satisfaction when it is over. I am not an exhibitionist, as most murderers are. It will be enough for me to know that I have achieved what so many have attempted unsuccessfully. My whole life is lived inwardly—all my triumphs and failures are secret things and this will be the same. I have a mask, as we all have, and it is an excellent one for its purpose for behind it I can go my way and think and do what I please.

What shall I feel, I wonder, if by chance someone has such an obvious motive for killing my victim that he is at once suspected? If, moreover, it is someone here in Selby-on-Sea who cannot account for his movements at the time of the crime? It is really quite probable. Perhaps he will be arrested, tried and eventually executed. What will be my reaction to that? Amusement, on the whole. When I think what people have done to me, I am not going to break my heart about the death penalty being wrongfully carried out in yet another case. If they want to have a death penalty they must be prepared for a few misapplications of it.

But it is not likely to go as far as that. The most they will do is to suspect anyone with a motive—the case will never be solved. I am writing this only to clear my ideas and when I have finished I shall destroy it.

There are a few details which it may seem are being overlooked, but in fact I have considered them all. At one time I thought I might do something to make myself less recognizable on the night—strange clothes, dark glasses and some of the face covered. I have shelved the idea for several reasons. For one it is a complication, and these are to be avoided at all costs. For another it is unnecessary, for even if I pass someone who knows me it cannot implicate me. Also I should have to get rid of things—clothes, dark glasses and so on—afterwards, and that again means a possibility of leaving some clue where none exists. I shall probably be somewhat muffled up, but who would not be on the seafront on a winter's evening? No one not previously acquainted with me will be able to identify me from the little seen of me as I pass and if I meet anyone who recognizes me I shall stop and chat for a time. As simple as that.

I also thought of a dog. No one gains the confidence of strangers so easily in England as a dog-owner. Nothing would make my evening walk so innocent-seeming as a dog on a lead. But there are two things against it. It could be a means of identification because people notice a dog more than its owner. And it would be an elaboration. I may think again about this but at present I'm against it. I have also thought of sallying forth with a companion that night and on some pretext leaving him or her either for the rest of the evening or for sufficient time to carry out my plan. This has advantages and disadvantages and will have to be considered more closely.

Then as to time and opportunity. I have said I will wait for this, but I do not mean that I am going to haunt that last shelter on the seafront till the moment arrives. I shall observe it as far as I can when I take an evening stroll (which must not be too often) but if I find that I meet someone near there more than once, or if I am observed on that part of the promenade, I shall at once change my plans. No one must be able to come forward afterwards and say they have seen me in that direction. With any luck the circumstances will combine quickly, but if they don't I simply start again.

My visits in any case will not be at regular times. People in a place like this do everything at regular times, rise, eat, take walks and sleep. The chances are that one or two people take the air on the seafront every evening at six or eight, and if I made my visit a fixed thing we should get to know one another by sight. No, that must never happen. I shall go sometimes as early as seven and sometimes as late as eleven.

I shall wait till October is over and the last of the autumn visitors have gone, then, on one of those dark blustering November or December nights I shall know the delicious sensation of being a murderer. . . .

2

THE Queen Victoria hotel at Selby-on-Sea was not, as its advertisements claimed, two minutes from the beach, unless you had a fast motor-car and there was no traffic, but six minutes' sharp walking brought you from its stolid façade down Carter Street to the seafront. It was not the best hotel in Selby, but it was by no means the worst, a frowsty place of comfortable chairs and big bed-rooms in which the furniture and fittings had not been changed since the hotel opened in the year of the Diamond Jubilee. Once the bourn of commercial travel-lers it still catered for visitors on business rather than holiday-makers for there was nothing very festive about its dining-room, which overlooked a narrow street, or its lounge from the lace-curtained windows of which could be caught no glimpse of the sea.

Its bar had an entrance direct from the street and was a popular meeting-place for the town's residents, particu-larly in winter when a big coal fire was lit half an hour before opening. There was a vast mahogany erection of mirrors and cornices and between this and the counter were to be seen two ladies who had presided there for several years and were known as Doris and Vivienne.

They were admirably contrasted, Vivienne tall, remote, pensive and pale, Doris short, talkative, given to whispered conferences with clients across the bar, Doris leaning over and the customer stretching forward till their heads were close together. These conferences had a way of being terminated with a sentence or two for all to hear. Whisper, whisper, whisper the two would go until suddenly both participants would stand upright and Doris would say loudly—" So you see, don't you? " or " I only hope you're right," as though to indicate that there had been no secrets. Perhaps there had not and Doris's conspiratorial behaviour was a mannerism.

Everyone liked Doris, but it was Vivienne to whom they turned when they became pot-valiant and talkative, for her hauteur tempted them. Doris would smile to all the customers but to win a smile from the cold thin lips of Vivienne was an achievement. Both ladies were in their late thirties and both were described by the hotel's proprietor as ' smart-looking girls ', but Vivienne's languid expression made her seem older than dumpy, cheerful Doris.

" Nasty blustering night, isn't it? " said Doris to Vivienne when they opened the bar one evening in late November.

" Mmmm," said Vivienne musically. It was not exactly a word, but it was more than a letter. Humming through several notes it was absent-minded, yet perfectly polite, and with various modulations served Vivienne for most forms of discourse.

" Shouldn't like to have to go out this evening. The wind seems to go right through you."

" Oh, I don't know," reflected Vivienne.

" I thought so as I came in. It cuts through you like a knife, I thought. There weren't many about, either. You can't blame them. Just one or two on the front."

" Mmmm? "

" Yes. I noticed as I came by. I thought to myself, I wonder whatever they want to walk along there for on an evening like this. I suppose it's sea air they're after. Well, there's enough of it to go round. Did you enjoy the film? "

" Mmmm," said Vivienne dubiously.

" They're a long time starting to come in tonight, aren't they? There's no one much in the hotel. One booked in just now, though. I saw him as I was coming through the hall."

"Mmmm?" said Vivienne with slightly more animation.

"Yes. Kind of staring eyes. Didn't look as though he was much, either. One little case and rather shabby-looking, I thought. I expect he'll be in later and you can see for yourself. Perhaps you'll fancy him!"

"Mmmm!" denied Vivienne disdainfully.

They were busy for the next half-hour with the regulars, Vivienne for all her remoteness as efficient in serving as Doris. Some intimate matter engaged Doris and Mr Lobbin, the newsagent, from a few doors away, for their heads were close for several minutes, to be separated finally with Doris's loud—"I'd never have believed it, mind you." The windy cheerless night seemed to have driven in more than usual of the town's sturdy business-men and there was a discreet bass rumble of hearty talk.

Presently Doris moved close to Vivienne as she poured a Guinness.

"That's the fellow I told you about. Standing near the door. The one who booked in tonight. Got a funny look, hasn't he?"

"Mmmm," said Vivienne not without interest.

"I don't like those eyes, though. The sort you read about in the paper. Seem to drill right into you, don't they? That's his second double Scotch in ten minutes."

The man she referred to was gaunt and grey-haired, a stringy individual with large powerful hands. He might have been fifty, or a little less. His mouth was wide but thin-lipped and tightly shut and his eyes, as Doris said, were large and staring. He seemed to take no notice of anyone but drank as though it was a timed exercise, a gulp, a wait, a gulp and then two or three steps to the bar for a refill.

Doris could not take her eyes from him.

"I don't like it," she said to Vivienne. "There's something queer about him. Look at the way he's drinking that whisky as though he'd got a train to catch. Glad I don't

13

sleep in the hotel. I shouldn't have a moment's peace thinking about it."

"Oh well," volunteered Vivienne chattily.

"You don't think he's escaped from Somewhere, do you? He might have, you know. I was only reading in the paper the other day . . ."

At this point the man under discussion came up to the bar.

"Where's the telephone?" he asked.

"There isn't one, not in the bar," exclaimed Doris. "You'll have to go through to the hall. You'll see it there. It's got 'Telephone' up on it. You'll need coppers, though, because it's a public box. Did you want a local call?"

The man hesitated.

"Yes," he said at last.

"I can give you coppers if you want them."

Without answering the man went towards the door leading to the hall.

"There," said Doris. "I told you there was something funny about him. Did you notice the way he looks at you with those eyes? Seem to go right into you. Didn't it give you a queer feeling?"

"Mmmm," said Vivienne, dubiously negative.

"Well it did me. Soon as ever I saw him. I hope he doesn't come back in here. He's had four doubles already." She turned to a customer. "Yes, Mr Stringer? A nice light ale? There was something I was going to tell you." She was soon leaning forward while Mr Stringer, torn between her whisper and his thirst, uneasily inclined his head. After he had taken a long draught, he began to nod appreciatively and in his turn to reply. "So it wasn't what it looked like being, was it?" said Doris at last releasing him.

It was at least ten minutes before the man returned and ordered another large Scotch, served in silence by Vivienne.

"Did you get through?" asked Doris chattily.

"No. No reply from any of them," said the man.

"There. Isn't it a nuisance when you want to call someone and there's no answer? Still, you can try again later, can't you? You staying long?"

"I don't know yet."

"It's a bit quiet this time of year. I mean, look at the weather. You can't expect people to come to the seaside when it's like this. It's not raining though, is it? Just dark and blowy. Still, you're all right. You're staying in the hotel. You haven't got to go out in it."

"Who says I haven't?" he asked rather fiercely.

"Well of course I don't know. I only thought that as you were staying in the hotel . . ."

"Give me another Scotch."

Doris seemed subdued for a moment as she served him. It was the man who spoke again.

"I've got business to attend to here," he said.

"I thought you must have," said Doris. "No one comes much in the winter otherwise."

The man's large eyes, which had an expression of resentment but of anxiety or even fear too, watched Doris fixedly, but she thought they showed a certain glazed haziness. The whisky so steadily swallowed was beginning to have its effect. When he next spoke he used a surprising phrase.

"I'm presumed dead," he said.

Doris tried a startled giggle.

"Whatever do you mean?" she asked. "You're alive enough."

"*Presumed* dead," said the man impatiently. "Have been for years though I did not know it. How would you like to be presumed dead?"

"I don't know what you mean," said Doris uncomfortably.

"When nothing's heard of you after a time your family can consider you a dead man. That's what I mean. I've been a dead man for years. Now I'm coming to life again."

"That's a funny way to talk," said Doris.

"I'll tell you something else," said the man. "There's more than one in this town who won't be at all pleased

15

at my resurrection." A very unpleasant smile appeared on his face. "They won't be at all pleased."

"Do you know it well?" asked Doris, aiming at normal talk. "Selby-on-Sea, I mean?"

"Never been here before in my life," said the man, motioning to show he wanted yet another whisky. "But I've . . . blood ties with it, you might say."

"You do say funny things," said Doris, looking anything but amused.

"And I do funny things, too," the man told her. "Especially to those who do funny things to me."

He moved away from the counter and Doris watched him find a place in a far corner of the room.

"He gives me the creeps," she confided to Vivienne. "I don't know what he's on about half the time, death and resurrection and that."

"Religious, perhaps," said Vivienne indifferently as she served a small gin-and-pep.

"It's not that," said Doris. "Presumed dead, was what he told me and now he's come to life again. He says some won't be pleased at that, and I don't wonder."

"Mmmm," agreed Vivienne absently on two notes.

"When George comes in to do the fire I'm going to ask him to see what name that fellow's given in the hall. Sounded so funny about people in the town not being pleased to see him. I'd like to know who he is."

George duly appeared at nine o'clock and was sent on his mission. He came back to tell Doris that the new guest's name was Ernest Rafter.

"Can't say I've ever heard it," Doris regretfully told Vivienne. "It's not one of the regular customers anyway. That's not saying it isn't known in the town, though."

Vivienne somehow thought she'd heard the name but couldn't remember where. She did not sound interested.

Half an hour later the man called Ernest Rafter brought his glass to the counter but did not order another drink. He moved with the peculiar deliberateness of one who is controlling his own tipsiness.

"I shall leave it till tomorrow," he told Doris

ambiguously. "Plenty of time then. I don't feel like tackling it tonight."

"Going to bed, are you? That's right. You get a nice night's sleep and you'll feel better tomorrow."

"I am not going to bed. I don't need a nice night's sleep and I feel perfectly well tonight," retorted the man sulkily.

"You do whatever you think best, then. I was only saying."

"I shall go for a walk," said Ernest Rafter obstinately.

"What, in all that wind? It cuts right through you like a razor. Wherever are you going?"

"Promenade," said the man. "There is a promenade, isn't there?"

"Of course there is. Ever so nice it is in summer. But there won't be many out there tonight."

"Suits me. Good night."

"Cheerio," said Doris and watched him march resolutely to the door. "He's had too much," she told Vivienne. "I can't think what he's going down to the front for, unless it's to cool his head. He'll certainly do that in this wind, won't he?"

"Mmmm," said Vivienne, agreeing.

Meanwhile Ernest Rafter made straight for the sea as though he went to an appointment. His light raincoat did little to protect him from the wind and his head and shoulders were thrust forward. He passed almost no one on his way down Carter Street which ran from the Queen Victoria hotel to the promenade, not even a policeman trying doors or a conscientious drinker coming from his pub. One bundle of rather aged womanhood and a young man with hands in pockets ostentatiously without a coat were the only people he saw and of these he took no notice.

"Tomorrow," he said irritably and aloud, as he reached the promenade. It was as though he was answering someone's nagging questions. 'Tomorrow,' he was thinking. 'There's plenty of time. They'll have to pay for my hotel. Might even stay for a while.'

Had he been sober enough for surprise he would have found it odd that the asphalt was not quite deserted. Even by the reduced lighting he could see several hurrying figures and coming towards him was a young policeman who had evidently just completed a tour of inspection of the promenade. The policeman seemed to eye him rather fixedly but said nothing as he passed.

Ernest Rafter breathed heavily. The cold wind seemed to make his head swim and he hesitated, as though trying to decide which direction to take, to the left towards the bandstand or to the right, towards the end of the promenade and the last shelter. He chose the right.

As he walked he was passed more than once but was almost unaware of it and certainly had no idea what sort of being had gone by. On the contrary he believed himself alone, but he was accustomed to that. He had no friends and wanted none. More than half drunk but obstinately determined to complete the walk he had undertaken, he pushed forward against the wind. He passed several shelters which seemed to offer a respite from his drunken battle with the elements, but resisted the temptation to sit down.

It was not until he came to the last shelter, curiously isolated it seemed, that he felt at last he must rest. He was just sober enough to choose a seat on the lee side. In a few moments he was in a cramped and stertorous sleep.

3

THE policeman whom Ernest Rafter had passed was called Sitwell and had been on the promenade beat for about a fortnight. He was an ambitious and idealistic young man who believed in the high purpose of law and order and saw himself and his fellow policemen as avenging angels in a population conveniently divided into black and white, cops and robbers. He longed to catch a criminal.

Leaving the promenade he made his way over to the bottom of Carter Street. He did not ascend it, however, but followed the row of shops facing the sea and conscientiously tried door-handles as he passed. He did not hurry, having been taught to adopt the slow, swinging pace of the policeman. An hour later he returned to the promenade for his second tour of inspection.

There were times, he had to admit, when he was depressed by the law-abiding dullness of Selby-on-Sea. He had been here six months and except for one disturbance outside a public house in which he had intervened successfully, there had been no opportunity for him to distinguish himself. Not even the public lavatories had provided him with a conviction and the only time he had found a car where parking was forbidden it had earned him a reprimand, for it belonged to a local magistrate notably sympathetic to police evidence in court. To a young man burning with the ambition to bring evil-doers to the bar of justice it was discouraging.

Each day he read in his newspaper of the 'crime wave' which seemed to rampage everywhere but in Selby-on-Sea. Hold-ups, warehouse robberies, wage-snatches, arson, murder and general mayhem were all over the country except in the town to which he, Graham Sitwell, had been posted. He began to think he would end his days as an old station tea-drinker with nothing to show for his enthusiasm but a couple of liquor-out-of-hours convictions, a few queers and exhibitionists sentenced and the usual motoring offences brought to book.

Take tonight, for instance. It should be a promising one, by all fictional standards, a blustering wind along a half-lit promenade deserted except by a few hardy visitors. The ideal setting for a crime, yet what chance was there?

Just for a moment an hour ago when he had passed that man with the staring eyes who looked as though he was half cut, Sitwell's hopes had risen. A strange-looking

19

creature, that had seemed, apparently undecided as to what to do. But the man had marched on, his pace un-wavering. It was always like that, Sitwell's potential baby-snatchers, rapists or screwsmen turned out to be harmless citizens on their way home.

There were several pedestrians on the promenade, which was surprising since it was a quarter to eleven and an angry night, but Sitwell was sure he would know most of them by sight.

Here for instance came Lobbin, the newsagent, a large ungainly man reputed to be bullied by his wife. The poor chap had probably come out for a brief escape from her. He wore a thick scarf and had his hand up to hold on to his hat as he passed Sitwell but not, the policeman thought, with any idea of being unrecognized. He did not say good evening but that meant nothing as Sitwell had done no more than go into his shop in civvy clothes. But Sitwell turned after Lobbin had passed and, as though looking out to sea, watched him from the corner of his eye till he had crossed the road and disappeared in the direction of his shop. Sitwell resumed his slow, dignified walk in the direction of the farthest shelter.

He saw a man and woman coming towards him but as they drew nearer he failed to recognize them. The woman was the taller of the two and though Sitwell could not see much of her face he thought there was something mannish in her gait and build. Trained to observe, he looked down at her feet and thought they were unusually large, but decided that the half light was deceiving. They had certainly not passed him on any of his previous visits to the promenade, tonight or on other nights. They did not speak as they went by—scarcely surprising in this wind. He passed a fair-haired hatless youth, then reached the Public Lavatory, but it was locked for the night. Between it and the most distant shelter of the promenade there was only one other shelter, near which the road ceased to run beside the promenade and curved inland, leaving a V of public garden, also locked at night. It was his misfortune, he reflected, to come on duty after these two otherwise promising venues for law-breaking were closed to the public.

He caught up with a little plump man who was walking very slowly and looking out to sea. He had seen this man on other evenings, always walking rather briskly. Tonight it was either the wind against him which made him dawdle or perhaps something out at sea which had caught his attention. He passed him and with his long strides soon left him behind. Now no one was visible ahead between him and the farthest shelter which was the limit of his beat.

Considering the matter afterwards he decided that it was instinct, the instinct of a shrewd policeman, which made him examine the last shelter by the light of his torch instead of turning back gratefully to have the wind behind him. He saw the thing at once, of course. Someone asleep, he decided, and approached to give the sleeper a kindly shake and advice to go home. His hand was stretched out to do this when he realized with sudden mounting nausea that it was useless. The man on the shelter seat could not be woken. Or what was left of the man.

Sitwell's various realizations came one after another or simultaneously—he could never decide which, or in what order. He realized that the dead body before him was that of the man with staring eyes whom he had passed less than an hour ago. He realized that the top of his cranium was a bloody pulp. He saw a heavy hammer lying beside the man's feet which was presumably the weapon that had killed him. Above all, he realized with a kind of sick jubilation that he had come at last on an important crime.

For a few moments he stood looking down. The man had not slumped to the ground but was still in a huddled sitting posture, his head forward as though he were exhibiting the ghastly evidence of his smashed skull. His hands were still in the pockets of his raincoat. He appeared to have been struck suddenly and powerfully, perhaps while he was sleeping.

Action, thought Sitwell. Instant action—but what? He must not leave this, even for a moment. Yet he must inform the station at once. He must not touch anything here, or allow it to be touched. He was not perturbed by any doubt as to whether the man was dead—it was only too obvious. But what was he to do?

At that moment he saw someone coming from the direction in which he had himself approached. It was the little muffled up man he had passed a few minutes earlier.

Sitwell stepped out and stopped him before he came too near.

"Excuse me," he said. "Would you be kind enough to make a telephone call for me? There's a box at the corner of the street over there."

The muffled figure nodded.

"Would you ring the police station, Selby 2222, and tell them to send a car down here immediately?"

The muffled one seemed to hesitate as though expecting more information than this.

"Tell them that someone is dead," said Sitwell.

That was enough. The muffled figure hurried away.

Now, thought Sitwell, alone with his grisly find, I shall be able to give the exact information they always require. I passed this man at precisely . . .

He examined his watch. It was now 10.55 so it would be safe to give the time of his meeting with the man with the staring eyes as 9.40. Better make it 9.42—sounded more accurate. He made a note of that.

The man had then taken this direction, walking as though he was keeping himself under control. How had Sitwell known he had been drinking? He could only say he got that impression from the man's eyes when he had been standing there, having just come from the streets of the town.

Sitwell saw delightedly that he would also be able to supply precise information about the people he had met as he approached the shelter. Mr Lobbin he could certainly identify. 'Lobbin' he wrote. Then he remembered the man and woman. He would be able to demonstrate his keen powers of observation over that—the woman's large feet and mannish air. Would he be able to identify them if he saw them again? He thought so. Certainly if they were together.

What about those he had met during his earlier walk past this very shelter? He would carefully recall who they were. But his own movements, he thought, would fix the time of the murder to within an hour—it must have been committed between 9.50 say, and 10.40.

This was all very satisfactory. He would make an excellent witness when the murderer was eventually on trial and in the meantime his account to the CID men would surprise them by its accuracy. He began to see himself out of uniform almost immediately.

But suppose that little man did not phone? No one else might pass this way tonight and he dare not leave the corpse. Perhaps he could stop a car? Yes, that would be his move. Stop the first car that came by and ask it to take a report to the station.

It was soon obvious, however, that his messenger had fulfilled his function, for a police car drew up and Detective Inspector John Moore came towards him.

Sitwell was rather disappointed. Moore had only just come to Selby, transferred with promotion from the Buddington area. He seemed a quiet and efficient sort of person but not easily impressed. If it had been their last chief, Inspector Burton, he would have been ready to congratulate Sitwell and perhaps recommend his transfer to the CID. With this man it was impossible to tell.

" Accident? " he said sharply to Sitwell.

" No, sir. Murder."

Moore gave him a quick and none-too-friendly look as much as to say that it was not for the uniformed branch to make analyses.

Sitwell watched Moore, a burly fellow in his early forties, approach the corpse. He made no move to touch it but gave it a careful scrutiny. His eyes went to the hammer on the floor.

" Anyone touched that? " he asked.

" Not since I arrived," said Sitwell.

" When was that? "

" About ten minutes ago. I was making my second . . ."

" Yes, yes. Who has seen this? "

" To my knowledge no one. There can't have been much time. I had passed this man earlier . . ."

" How do you know? "

" I recognize him, sir."

Moore grunted, perhaps incredulously.

" You'll make out a full statement presently. For goodness sake get your *times* right and don't exaggerate their accuracy. Better to say ' about such a time ' than pretend you noticed to a minute. Time's going to be all-important here. Anyone about when you came along? "

" I passed several people. I . . ."

" Give me all those details in your report. There was no one near this shelter that you saw? "

" No, sir."

" And you found the dead man exactly like that? "

" Yes. I've touched nothing."

" Know who he is? "

" No. I've never seen him before this evening. I gained the impression he'd been drinking."

" Oh. You gained the impression. What did you gain it from? "

" His eyes, for one thing. The way he walked . . ."

" Falling about? "

" No. He seemed to be controlling himself."

Moore nodded.

" I know. He was alone, of course? "

" Yes."

" Coming from? "

" The town. I met him just as I was leaving the prom to go towards Carter Street."

" Speak? "

" No. He stood there a moment as though he could not make up his mind. That would have been at about ten to ten."

" Until you found him here you had noticed nothing? "

" I noticed everything," said Sitwell in a hurt tone.

" I mean, nothing unusual. No sound? No one behaving in any noticeable way? "

" No, sir. Nothing like that. It was just a windy night with very few about."

" What made you chance on him? "

" It was a sort of instinct. As I came up to this shelter I kind of felt something. It may have been coincidence but . . ."

" It was. You just made your routine check with a torch? "

" Well, yes sir. Then I saw this . . ."

" Right. You remain here till they all come down, photographers, finger-print boys and the doctor. Touch nothing and let no one come anywhere near. They won't be long."

" Very well, sir."

" Then go and make a full report before you go off duty. Everything you can remember. Everyone you saw. All the details you can manage. Your report may be important. I want facts, not theories. We'll do all the theorizing and it looks to me as though we'll have to do quite a lot."

There was silence for a minute and both men looked down at the dead thing on the seat.

" You say this was the second time you came to this shelter this evening. What time were you here before? "

" Must have been about 9.30."

" Anyone here? "

" No, sir. I'm quite definite about that. I always take a good look at this place. It seems . . ."

" Yes. Who phoned the station? "

" A passer-by. I called to this little man . . ."

" *What* little man? What was his name? "

" I didn't ask him."

" You didn't *ask* him? He was round this shelter and you didn't even take a note of his name? "

" He was coming towards it."

" But you'd know him again? "

" He was all muffled up."

John Moore's comment was violent and profane and he left Sitwell wondering whether after all he had chosen the right career.

4

A FORTNIGHT later Detective Inspector John Moore drove over to Newminster where an old friend of his, Carolus Deene, taught history at the Queen's School. His object, he assured himself, was to go over the problem with Deene and in doing so, in giving coherence to his thoughts in the matter as he stated his case, perhaps gain a clearer idea of it.

It would not be the first time he had talked over such things with Carolus, for he had been stationed in New-minster when, as a very young man, he was transferred to the CID and made his first investigations. Carolus then had just been Released and although an uncomfortably rich man had taken up a teaching appointment rather than be idle. His girl wife had been killed in an air raid and Carolus, a lonely young widower, wanted occupation.

The Queen's School, Newminster, is, as its pupils find themselves under the necessity rather often of explaining, a public school. A minor, a small, a lesser-known one, they concede, but still in the required category. Its buildings are old, picturesque and very unhygienic, and one of its classrooms is a showpiece untouched from the Eliza-bethan age in which the school was founded.

Some years before this time the school had been given a little reflected fame, for Carolus Deene published a success-ful book and did not scorn to print under his name ' Senior History Master at the Queen's School. Newminster '. The book was called *Who Killed William Rufus? And Other Mysteries of History*, and in it Deene most ingeniously applied the methods of a modern detective to some of the more spectacular crimes of the past and in more than one case seemed to have found new evidence from which to draw startling conclusions.

On the Princes in the Tower he was particularly original and perceptive and he disposed of much unreliable detail in his study of the murder of Edward II. The book was highly praised and sold a number of editions.

" It doesn't, unfortunately, make Deene a good disciplinarian," said the headmaster. " His class is the noisiest rabble in the school."

Carolus Deene was forty years old. He had been a good, all-round athlete with a half-blue for boxing and a fine record in athletics. During the war he did violent things, always with a certain elegance for which he was famous. He jumped out of aeroplanes with a parachute and actually killed a couple of men with his Commando knife which, he supposed ingenuously, had been issued to him for that purpose.

He was slim, dapper, rather pale and he dressed too well for a schoolmaster. He was not a good disciplinarian as the headmaster understood the word, because he simply could not be bothered with discipline, being far too interested in his subject. If there were stupid boys who did not feel this interest and preferred to sit at the back of his class and eat revolting sweets and hold whispered conversations on county cricket, then he let them, continuing to talk to the few who listened. He was popular but considered a little odd. His dressiness and passionate interest in both history and crime were his best-known characteristics in the school, though among the staff his large private income was a matter for some invidious comment.

The boys were apt to take advantage of his known interest in crime both ancient and modern. A master with a hobby-horse is easily led away from the tiresome lesson in hand into the realms of his fancy. He may or may not realize this as the end of the school period comes and he finds that he has talked for three-quarters of an hour on his favourite subject and forgotten what he was supposed to be teaching.

Carolus Deene was very well aware of his weakness but he regarded his twin interests of crime and history as almost indistinguishable. The history of men is the history of their crimes, he said. Crippen and Richard III, Nero and the latest murderer to be given headlines in newspapers were all one to him, as his pupils delightedly discovered.

Carolus lived in a small Queen Anne house hidden, with its charming walled garden, in the old part of the town. He was looked after by a married couple named Stick who had been with him for a good many years and threatened to leave him every time he became involved in what Mrs Stick called 'nasty police cases'. She was a formidable little woman, an inspired cook and housekeeper, but so stiff with respectability that she suffered every time Carolus had a caller of whom she disapproved.

When John Moore reached the house that December evening she recognized him at once.

" Mr Deene's out," she said curtly.

" At the school? "

" I couldn't say, I'm sure," said Mrs Stick, peering at Moore closely through her steel-rimmed spectacles.

" I'd better go over there," suggested Moore.

" You'd better do nothing of the sort. Mr Deene mustn't be disturbed while he's teaching."

" Oh, that will be all right, Mrs Stick. He knows me."

" I daresay he does, but it's not to say he wants policemen running round under his feet when he's giving his lessons."

" Shall I wait for him then? "

Mrs Stick was torn between unpleasant alternatives but at last said, " I suppose you'd better." She stood aside for him. " You wipe your feet though and don't bring all that mud into my clean hall."

When Moore was sitting by the fire she brought him a tray of drinks.

" It wouldn't be a policeman if he didn't want these,"

she reflected aloud. " I hope you're not going to start dragging Mr Deene into any more cases, are you? We had quite enough after that last one."

" No. I've just come to talk over something and hear his views."

" You know what that will mean. Off he'll go again and we shan't know from day to day what murders he may be mixed up in. I was only saying to Stick . . ."

They heard the front door and in a moment Carolus was with them and greeting Moore.

" I'm glad to see Mrs Stick has been looking after you," he said with some amusement while the little woman was still in the room.

" It was only to stop him racing round the school showing everyone what company you keep," said Mrs Stick. " What would the headmaster say, I'd like to know, if he found a policeman come to get you? "

" He hasn't come to get me, Mrs Stick. Only—unless I'm mistaken?—to have a little chat about Selby-on-Sea."

" So that's it! I read about it in the paper. As soon as I saw it my heart jumped into my mouth. I said to Stick, I said, ' It's to be hoped Mr Deene doesn't get himself mixed up in this,' I said, ' or who's to say *he* won't have someone after him with a coal-hammer, same as that poor fellow did.' If I'd known that's what this was about I'd never have let him over the threshold."

" Stay and have something to eat, John? What have we, Mrs Stick? "

" I don't know whether there'll be enough. I'm not saying I couldn't do a little extra of the eggs if it comes to it. It's the thought of you sitting here talking about all this nastiness."

" I'm sure you can manage it."

" I suppose I shall have to. There's oafs arler die able and patty der gibyer, if you want to know. And I've got up a bottle of the Montrashy. But how I'll be able to cook, knowing what I do, I can't bear to think."

" *Oeufs à la diable*, devilled eggs and *pâté de gibier*,

game pie," translated Carolus. "Very nice and very appropriate, Mrs Stick."

Her face showed no appreciation of this praise as she left the two men.

"Now, John, tell us all about it," said Carolus.

"It's a bastard, this one," began Moore. "Nothing to get hold of at all."

"No motive?"

"Bags of motive. But nothing to connect any of those who had motive with the crime." Carolus waited. "This man Ernest Rafter who was killed had only arrived in Selby that afternoon. He'd been staying in a lodging-house near King's Cross station. He was a pretty bad hat, I gather."

"In what way?"

"Collaborator," said Moore.

For both of them this was sufficient, for they belonged to a generation of men among whom these things were not forgotten.

"Japs?"

"Yes. It's an old story and I've been through the MI 5 files. He was so useful to the Japanese that they took the trouble to protect him from his fellow-prisoners who would certainly have knocked him off. So the Japs gave out that he had been shot trying to escape and moved him to another camp under another name. He was reported missing believed killed and in due course his family got him officially presumed dead."

"I see. And his family live in Selby-on-Sea?"

"Most of them, yes. It's a large family."

"Money involved?"

"Yes. Some. The father died soon after the war and left a few thousands, divided equally among his three sons and two daughters. The murdered man's share has long since gone to the others."

"So that if he had turned up alive?"

"He would have had no legal claim, I gather, but a very strong moral one. Besides it would have been an infernal nuisance to them all. One of the brothers is a solicitor and none of them was likely to welcome this Ernest."

"You say a moral obligation. Are they the kind of people who would have recognized that?"

"I should say certainly. They're supposed to be a bit close, I believe, but quite honourable."

"Then hardly the kind of people to have killed him with a hammer?"

"Well, no. But, as we both know, there is no 'kind of people' for murder. These are the only ones known to have a motive of any sort and most of them, perhaps all of them, were in the town that night."

"I see."

"We've traced Rafter's movements. The name he took when he was in Japanese hands was Randle. After the war he succeeded in reaching Australia and bummed his way around there till a few months ago. He must have known his father was dead but the old man was a bit of a miser. No one thought he had more than a few hundred pounds to leave and I suppose Rafter didn't think it worth while admitting his identity for that. His collaboration was rather a famous one in its way. He might even have been charged with war crimes."

"Or treason."

"Then I suppose he got news of what had happened or he was desperate. At all events he came home. Reached London two weeks before he came down to Selby."

"Oh. Two weeks. Then he may have been in communication with the family?"

"They all deny this. They all say they had heard or seen nothing to make them doubt that he was dead. He certainly went to Somerset House and saw his father's will. He came down to Selby on the 4.15 that day and put up at the Queen Victoria. He went into the bar, knocked back half a dozen doubles and told one of the barmaids he had been presumed dead and that his 'resurrection' would not be welcomed by certain people in the town. Then, although it was a beastly night with a cold wind, he insisted on taking a walk on the promenade."

"There is nothing to suggest that he had spoken to any of the family then?"

"Nothing. He asked to use the telephone and came back to the bar to say he could not get through. His movements otherwise don't leave much opportunity. His train got in on time at 5.40 and he went straight to the Queen Victoria. He went up to his room for a wash and was in the bar by half past six or so. He did not leave it, except when he tried to telephone, till 9.30 or thereabouts. Then he walked straight down to the promenade, passing a man on his beat at about twenty to ten. At 10.50 our man found him dead in the farthest shelter—right at the end of the promenade."

"Had he got his wits about him, this man of yours?"

Moore smiled.

"An enthusiast, anyway. Rather turned his head, having found the corpse. Sitwell, his name is and he's still in his early twenties. Thinks I'm pretty unappreciative. But he seems to have got his times right, which is the main thing."

"I gather it was done with a sledge hammer."

"Oh no. That's press exaggeration. It was a good heavy hammer such as is used for breaking coal, but not so big that it could not have been carried to the place unnoticeably by man or woman. It's the sort of thing that might be found in any house. Nothing of the sort has been reported missing or stolen. We're unlikely to trace its ownership, for it might be ten years old or more and thousands of them are sold all over the country."

"Finger prints?"

"Not one."

"Anything left anywhere near the body?"

"Nothing really. The technical boys have got some threads and particles, I believe, but they could only be any use as additional evidence if we had our man, and would be dubious then. Rafter apparently never took his hands out of his pockets so he wasn't clutching that traditional piece of cloth. Once we've found someone it is possible that the microscope will help, but it tells us nothing useful now."

" Is it certain that the man had been killed with the hammer? "

" As far as expert opinion goes, yes."

" At least you've got the time narrowed down nicely. How far was it from where Rafter passed the policeman to the shelter? "

" At the most fifteen minutes' walk for a man with drink in him and the wind against him. It could be done in ten."

" So the earliest possible time, if your man is accurate, is 9.50. And the latest, say 10.40. That's a very small margin, John."

" Yes. But what's the good of it? "

" Do you know who was along that part of the promenade at the time? "

" We know one or two. Our man unfortunately let one get away."

John Moore told Carolus of Sitwell's observations, including his meeting with Lobbin, whom Moore described as a very good chap.

" We've traced the woman with large feet, and her husband. She certainly would look rather mannish beside him at night. Their name's Bullamy and they're visitors to the town. We also know the man Lobbin, a local newsagent. But we can't trace a man Sitwell sent to the phone. Small, fat and muffled up is all I can get from him. Sitwell's a keen young man and annoyed with himself for not having seen the man properly and asked his name. He was so anxious to get someone to put a call through that he let this go. He remembers a young man without a hat or overcoat whom he saw on his second visit to the promenade. There are also a few people whom Sitwell saw earlier, but I'm only giving you the gist of the thing now. The real point seems to me that none of Rafter's family, no one in fact who could have the smallest motive so far as we know, was seen on the promenade that evening."

33

"Unless one of the two unidentified ones, the fat muffled man or the youth, belonged to the family."

"Exactly. We're checking on that, of course."

"Had the body been robbed?"

"Not unless it was some special object. Rafter had seven pounds in his pocket-case and a good watch."

"Have another drink, John. Mrs Stick won't be ready for us yet and I want to hear about the family."

"Thanks. First there's his elder brother Bertrand. About fifty, quiet, apparently quite unperturbed about the whole thing. He's a widower with a pleasant flat overlooking the sea. Good war record—temporary Colonel. Make no bones about it, he hoped never to see his brother again and truly believed him dead."

"Live alone?"

"There was a rather handsome girl there when I went, referred to as 'my secretary'."

"Then?"

"An unmarried sister. Emma Rafter. Horsey type. Cheerful, rather downright. She seems almost amused at being questioned. Then there's another sister with two sons, one grown up, a Mrs Dalbinney. Living apart from her husband but not divorced. A bit *grande dame* but apparently quite an ordinary sort of matron."

"What about the grown-up son?"

"I haven't met him yet. I gather he's clever. I believe the younger son, a boy of fifteen or so, is in your school here."

"I never know their names," admitted Carolus. "Is that all?"

"There is another brother, the only one, it seems, who does any work. He's a solicitor in Bawdon, our county town. Wife younger than he is and three small children."

"Not a very promising lot, John. But I see your point. Motive's the only wear. Can they all 'account for their movements', as they say, at the time of the crime?"

"Oh yes. They were quite good-natured about it. Spoke as though they were indulging me in a whim when I asked them. Bertrand had gone to bed. Emma and Mrs Dalbinney went together to the pictures and afterwards back to Mrs Dalbinney's flat for a nightcap. Emma stayed the night there as they were both alone. I haven't see the solicitor yet. He had been to see his sister in Selby that afternoon. I feel sure he'll be able to say exactly where he was."

"You're not regarding these as alibis, are you?"

"No. I haven't got so far. There would have to be a great deal of checking on them before we did that. But they sound perfectly reasonable."

"Have you tried to find anyone else with a motive for killing Ernest Rafter?"

"We're going into that now. All his movements since landing. A report's coming through from the Australian police, too. It may point to someone else. But he had come to the town to see his family."

"Yes. It's very, very tricky. From what you've already learned about him, would you say that Rafter might have been blackmailing anyone?"

"Not, strictly speaking, from what I've learnt. But it seems to me that a man who would collaborate almost voluntarily, before there was any sign of torture or anything of the sort, would do pretty well anything."

"I agree. I think we should know a great deal more about Ernest. The family doesn't sound promising."

"You've got no suggestions, Carolus?"

"On what you've told me, none at all. But I have a feeling that I may be spending Christmas in Selby-on-Sea."

Moore was silent.

"You know," he said presently. "If you do come you're on your own. This is a private chat, but if you're in the town you get no information from us. It has to be like that. I can't discuss the thing with you again."

"Of course I realize that."

"On the other hand I don't deny I shall be glad if you do come. We can't work together but this is a case where I'd be glad of one of your startling theories. I've got none at all at present, startling or otherwise. In fact there's only one thing certain in this case."

" And that? "

" It was murder. In other cases I've tackled it could be suicide or an accident. *This was murder.*"

" Yes, Mrs Stick? " said Carolus, for the little woman had come quietly into the room.

She glared at the two men, her lips tight and her small figure drawn up taut.

" Your dinner, sir," she brought herself to say.

Neither Carolus nor John discussed the matter which interested them till they were back in the study with their brandy and cigars.

Then Carolus said—" You mentioned some people seen by your man. Any of them interesting? "

Moore smiled.

" Interesting? You don't know Selby in winter. It's a parish pump sort of place. He saw four people in all, at least according to his report, and knew them all quite well. There was the Vicar of one of the town's four churches, the Reverend Theo Morsell and his wife."

Carolus sighed.

" There's always a parson," he said. " Who else? "

" Character called Bodger. Sort of professional Old Salt. Takes the visitors out in his boat in the summer. Troublesome but nothing serious known against him. Little bits of trouble, I believe. If we're going to be far-fetched I would add that his son died on the Burma Road. But he says that he had never heard of Ernest Rafter and I don't for a moment disbelieve him. There was also a man called Stringer, an assistant in an ironmonger's shop."

" I must say I don't envy you, John. And there's been plenty of publicity given to the case, I don't quite see why. The coal hammer, perhaps. It's always some detail like that which appeals to public imagination. They'll leave it in your hands? "

" I think so. But I've got to produce what are oddly

called 'results' fairly soon. When does your school break up?"

"On December 19. Early this year. I'll be there on the 20th."

"You'd better stay at the Hydro. It's supposed to be the best hotel."

"What about the Queen Victoria? That's where Rafter stayed, isn't it?"

"Yes. It's possible. Old-fashioned commercial."

"It'll suit me. I'll book a room."

Carolus returned once more to the matter of the murder by asking a direct question on policy.

"What line are you working on, John? You must have the beginnings of a theory."

"Scarcely even that. But it's obvious that the murderer could not have been at that shelter by chance, or have met Rafter there by chance."

"Or killed him by chance."

"Of course not. Therefore Rafter must have gone there by appointment, probably made on the phone when he said he couldn't get through. I think if we had an idea whom he called we'd be on our way. So we've more or less got to concentrate on the family."

"I wish you luck," said Carolus enigmatically and the discussion was closed.

5

THE interest of Carolus Deene in the Selby-on-Sea murder was heightened next day when one of his pupils, a cheerful spluttering boy called Dalbinney, came to him in the Break just as Carolus was hurrying to the masters' common room.

"Excuse me, sir. Could I ask you something?"

Not one of these keen youngsters, Carolus prayed, with a question arising out of the morning's history hour.

"Well?" he said discouragingly.

"You go in for detection, don't you, sir?"

By now, Carolus thought, his favourite chair and *The Times* crossword would have been appropriated by Hollingbourne, who would be writing in ink the two clues he usually got wrong.

"Well?" he said again.

This curtness seemed to reduce the boy to the greatest confusion.

"You see, sir, I live at Selby-on-Sea. I thought . . . you see my mother . . ."

Light dawned.

"Your name's Dalbinney, isn't it?"

"Yes, sir. That's why I thought . . . you see, it appears that the bumped-off man . . . my mother says . . ."

"Oh your prophetic soul! Your uncle," said Carolus rather fatuously.

"Well, yes, sir, I suppose he was. I mean I'd never heard of him . . . except that he died in the war . . . my mother thinks . . ."

"Does she? That's unusual for a mother."

"No, but I mean I told her . . . you see, she's read your book . . . she's coming to see you."

"Let's get this straight. You told your mother I had the misfortune to teach you."

"Yes, you see the police . . . I mean it being her long-lost brother . . . so I wrote and explained."

"That's more than you seem able to do now. What did you explain?"

"About you going in for crime. . . ."

"But I don't."

"Investigating I mean and all that . . . because my uncle . . ."

"Which uncle?"

"Bertrand. Uncle Locksley's a solicitor in Bawdon . . . only the police seem to think . . . because they're related you see . . . they've questioned mother already . . . so she's coming to see you."

"That seems to be the salient fact—your mother's coming to see me."

"Yes sir. Today I think it is . . . she's not worried or anything . . . only the police. . . ."

"This is where we came in," said Carolus firmly. "Thank you for warning me, Dalbinney."

He was right. Hollingbourne had written 'Lopper' for 'Does he make short work of things at the stern?' (6)'

"Nonsense," said Carolus looking over his shoulder. "'Docker', obviously."

"Thank you, Deene, for your brilliant intervention," said Hollingbourne with seething sarcasm. "But I happen to prefer my own interpretation. 'Short work' is clearly 'op'."

"Think so? What about 'the stern'?"

"Anagram of the remaining letters," said Hollingbourne huffily.

"LPER. What's the word?"

"Perl," said Hollingbourne, committed now. "Old term for the rudder of a ship."

"Your vocabulary's better than mine," said Carolus, adding "or than any lexicographer's. How's the wife?"

"Splendid, thank you. The baby's not expected till January. I saw young Dalbinney cornering you. I suppose he wants you in on this murder?"

"I couldn't quite gather what he wanted. 'Regal form of justice (5-5)' is 'King's Bench'."

"I think not. 'Royal Court' I fancy. Are you going to investigate the Selby murder?"

"I may spend Christmas down there. 'Royal Court' would upset 13 down. 'Low country relative' must be 'Dutch Uncle.'"

Hollingbourne handed Carolus *The Times.*

"You'd better do it, since you are so ingenious. The headmaster won't be pleased at your going to Selby."

"Not? Pity. What sort of boy is young Dalbinney?" said Carolus, busy correcting Hollingbourne's two entries.

"Very ordinary. The mother's a formidable woman."

"Indeed?"

"Formidable. She came to see me once about the elder son Paul who was in my house."

"Oh yes. He is now a young man in his twenties, I gather."

"Tiresome boy. I suggested extra coaching for him but his mother would not hear of it. Far too mean."

"Mean?"

"To a degree."

"How was the elder son tiresome?"

"Rowdy. Assertive. Precocious. A dangerous influence, I felt. Is he involved in this murder?"

"I don't know."

"Almost certainly I should think. He was extremely rude to my wife."

"I'm sorry to hear that."

"A lampoon, of sorts. In a diary he kept. Obscene, we considered it, though I have to admit it was not ill-written. He was intelligent. The younger brother is a better type altogether."

"More commonplace?"

"Much. Much," said Hollingbourne, conveying the highest praise he knew.

Mrs Dalbinney was waiting for Carolus when he reached his home after school that afternoon. It was evident from the manner of Mrs Stick when she met him in the hall that the name had conveyed nothing to her.

"There's a lady waiting to see you," she said with a suggestion of emphasis on the word 'lady'.

"Young, I hope?"

"I don't know about young, but she *is* a lady, which is more than I can say for some who have been here. Her son's at the school so I expect she has come to see you about his lessons. I'll bring the tea."

"Thank you, Mrs Stick. Yes, I expect that is what she has come for," said Carolus and went in to where Mrs Dalbinney had taken the chair in which John Moore sat yesterday.

Mrs Stick was right—she *was* a lady; so much so that she could not forget it for a moment. The rich intonations in her voice, the highly-tailored clothes and neat expensive jewellery, the quiet self-confidence all proclaimed it.

" I trust my son warned you that I meant to intrude on you this afternoon? " she said.

" Your son is not the most articulate of messengers but I managed to gather that."

Mrs Dalbinney smiled.

" I wish he had his brother Paul's brilliance," she said. " Peter is rather scatter-brained. But I haven't come to see you about him."

Mrs Stick entered with the tea-tray, and Carolus sought to avert a crisis by patter about it. Mrs Dalbinney would have a cup of tea, wouldn't she? In this cold weather. . . .

But Mrs Dalbinney was not to be deterred.

" I've come to see you about this terrible murder," she stated firmly.

For a moment Carolus thought the tray would be dropped. But Mrs Stick, with an air meant to indicate that the show must go on, managed to put it down on the appointed table. Her lips were tight as she left the room.

" It isn't that we feel any anxiety in the matter," said Mrs Dalbinney. " But it is highly unpleasant to have the police asking questions about one's movements at certain times. When I mentioned to my brothers and sisters what my son had told me about your successful intervention in several of such cases, we decided to enlist your aid. I may say that we are all in agreement about this. We want the sordid affair disposed of to relieve us of any further embarrassment."

" You can scarcely blame the police for questioning you," Carolus pointed out. " After all no one except his family could have wished this man out of the way. The police, quite rightly, have first to look for a motive."

" Oh, I don't blame them, Mr Deene. Not in the least. They have their duty. But to a family like *ours* it is very distressing and humiliating. You see we had *no* idea this unhappy brother was still alive. We had long since cast him out of our memories. And for him to be murdered on our very doorsteps was . . ."

" Inconsiderate? " suggested Carolus.

"If you put it like that. At all events we would like you to discover who murdered him."

Carolus considered. Then, remembering Hollingbourne's comment, for the first time in his life as an investigator he made an extraordinary statement.

"I'm afraid my fees are rather large," he said.

This took Mrs Dalbinney by surprise.

"I see. Of course. We shall be delighted. But I understood from my son that it was a hobby of yours."

"It is. But in this case I shall charge heavily."

Mrs Dalbinney's shoulders rose and fell in a discreet shrug.

"Of course if you need the money," she said.

"I don't. In fact when I get it I shall drive to the gates of Wormwood Scrubs prison and divide it, with no questions asked, between the men being released that morning."

"You put us in a difficult position. I am sure I speak for my family when I say we should not wish to help so unworthy, so ignoble a cause."

"Think so? Poor devils have had the world against them, whatever they've done."

"Your ideas of humanitarianism are curious and sentimental," pronounced Mrs Dalbinney. "But we want you to act for us."

"Then I will. I'll come to Selby-on-Sea on December the 20th, the day after the end of term."

"Won't that be too late?"

"For what?"

"No. I see. Of course not. We have nothing to fear. You will be with us for the holiday, then?"

"Yes. I'm sure you're all hoping for a white Christmas."

"You say most unaccountable things, Mr Deene. It cannot be much of a Christmas for us."

She rose and Carolus was surprised to find that she had not the stately figure one would have expected from her manner. She was in fact short and dumpy.

When she had gone Carolus waited rather apprehensively for Mrs Stick to come for the tea-tray. This, he considered, might really be the last straw and she would do what she had so often threatened—give notice.

But no. She looked fierce but said nothing. Was she at last becoming resigned?

Certainly, as he discovered next day, the headmaster of the Queen's School, Newminster, was becoming nothing of the sort.

Mr Gorringer, a large and important-looking man with a pair of huge crimson ears whose hairy cavities were marvellously attuned to passing rumour, had more than once found the peace of what he called the academic backwater of his school threatened by Carolus Deene. He considered that the incursions of his senior history master into the world of criminal investigation might bring 'unwelcome publicity in their train' and had tried with ponderous persuasiveness to divert the interests of Carolus.

That morning he took up his position at the large writing-table in his study and rang for the school porter, a disgruntled man named Muggeridge who resented the headmaster's insistence on a uniform which included a gold-braided silk hat.

He was a long time in answering the bell and when he came he said, " Yes? " in an aggrieved voice.

Mr Gorringer cleared his throat.

" Muggeridge," he said sternly, " I regret that I must again call attention to your mode of address. 'Yes, *sir*', or 'Good morning, sir', would become you better than a mere off-hand 'yes'."

" It's the Break," explained Muggeridge. " I was just having a cup of tea."

" I have no objection to that," conceded Mr Gorringer grandly. " However, to the matter in hand. Will you kindly ask Mr Deene to come here? It is urgent."

" If I can find him, I will. He sometimes nips home in the Break."

" That will do, thank you, Muggeridge."

Muggeridge went over to the masters' common room.

" He wants you," he told Carolus with an exasperated

sigh. "Sitting up there at his table like an assize judge. 'It's urgent', he said, though he only had to wait five minutes until after Break. I don't know."

But the headmaster, when Carolus entered, was loftily bland.

"Ah Deene," he said, "take a seat, pray. There is a small matter on which I wanted a Word with you."

"Mind if I smoke?"

"By all means." There was a long pause and a loud rumble while Mr Gorringer cleared his throat. "A little bird has whispered in my ear," he said and Carolus had a vision of a large vulture on the headmaster's shoulder, "that you are thinking of becoming embroiled in the investigation of a most sordid crime at Selby-on-Sea."

Hollingbourne, thought Carolus.

"I am thinking of spending Christmas there."

"Then rumour has not lied. I felt it my duty to point out to you that Selby-on-Sea is not a hundred miles from Newminster."

"No. It's twenty-two."

"And that we have more than one connection with the town. Apart from the danger of press publicity there may be a great deal of unwelcome talk if it becomes known that the senior history master of this school has become involved in anything so unpleasant as this. I gather that the murdered man was a wastrel, if no worse."

"He was the uncle of an old boy and of a boy now in Hollingbourne's house."

Mr Gorringer's protuberant eyes had a startled expression.

"You alarm me. Which boys?"

"Dalbinney P. W. and Dalbinney P. J."

"Dalbinney? I can scarcely credit it. I thought they came of an excellent family."

"It may be excellent but the whole lot of them are under suspicion. Including Dalbinney P. W., now a man of twenty and quite capable of wielding a coal-hammer."

"A coal-hammer? This is indeed a squalid story. You

44

are serious in telling me that a one-time pupil of ours is in the shadow of suspicion? And his uncle the victim of a brutal crime? "

" Why not? ' Death lays his icy hand on kings.' "

" This is a most regrettable business."

" He may not have done it, of course. Dalbinney P. W. I mean. He's only one of a number of suspects."

" You speak lightly, Deene. If you had the fair name of the school at heart you would take a more sober view. And you are actually considering a visit to this small seaside town? "

" The Dalbinneys' mother has asked me to investigate."

" More and more unfortunate. One of our most respected parents. I trust you will refuse? "

" I stuck out for a thumping big fee."

" I find that painful if not vulgar. I had no idea you charged money for your services. I supposed they were in the nature of a hobby."

" They are, often. But after what I've heard of this Mrs Dalbinney I've decided to make her and her family pay through the nose."

" Really, Deene. Your idiom is scarcely suited to an interview with your headmaster when in his official capacity."

" Anyway, I don't think you need feel much alarm on my account. My name won't be involved. If the school does come into it, it will be because of young Dalbinney."

" When do you intend to go? "

" As soon as we break up. On the 20th in fact."

" In view of Mrs Dalbinney's request I do not feel I should dissuade you as I had intended to do. I can only ask you to observe the greatest discretion. A coal-hammer, you say? "

" That was the weapon, apparently. The man was drunk, though, or something very like it."

Mr Gorringer gave a rather theatrical groan.

" I trust your first act will be to clear young Dalbinney from all suspicion. It is quite impossible that an old boy of the Queen's School, Newminster, should have killed his uncle with a coal-hammer."

"Nothing's impossible in crime, headmaster."

Carolus left Mr Gorringer at his desk, a somewhat baffled man, and hurried across to his classroom.

6

IT was with rather boyish exhilaration that Carolus drove his Bentley Continental towards Selby-on-Sea on the morning of December 20th. The term had finished with the school concert but he had escaped Mr Gorringer's annual dinner party for the staff. It was a crisp morning with pale sunlight thawing the frost on the bare hedges and he felt in splendid health and spirits.

He was going to an investigation which promised to be one of the most interesting he had known. All the circumstances suggested an intricate, teasing problem and a collection of odd human beings such as he liked to meet in the course of his enquiries. Moreover he would live with the crime, as it were, remaining in the town in which it had taken place, among the people involved in it. He felt like a schoolboy leaving for his first holiday abroad, knowing that everything he saw and heard would be of stirring interest to him.

Also, John Moore was in charge of police enquiries and though he would make no concessions or treat Carolus in any way but as an inquisitive member of the public, he would not impede Carolus and would always be ready to hear anything he might have to say.

There was, Carolus reflected, something very strange about this crime, something he could only sense which seemed to demand imagination and bold thinking. It was a premeditated murder, skilfully planned and executed. Yet there was no sign of anyone with a motive strong enough to inspire that kind of planning and execution and, on the face of it, the members of Rafter's family, the only people known to have a motive at all, sounded unlikely. John Moore could obviously do nothing but work on the supposition that one of them, man or woman, was responsible, at least until he discovered in Rafter's past an indication that the truth might lie elsewhere. Yet Carolus had a sort of instinct that this line of enquiry would lead to very little. Dangerous, he would have agreed, to have premature instincts of the kind before he had even met the people involved, but already he caught a whiff of something abnormal and hellish, something quite unconnected with the blunt straightforward murder of a man whose arrival from the past would bring unhappiness and financial loss to a number of respectable people. He had no idea what this something might be, but he did not think much of John Moore's makeshift beginnings of a theory.

Not that he would dismiss it so soon. He would meet this family and conscientiously consider each of them as the potential murderer, as he was bound to do. He would meet the other people seen on the promenade that night and everyone else who was in any way, however remotely, connected with the crime. Yet, he felt, his enquiries for a long time would be in the nature of almost aimless circling on the outer perimeter of the truth. Something would come from them, some hint be dropped, some fact emerge which might send him in an entirely different direction. That so often happened. He would be questioning A about B when A would say something apparently irrelevant which suddenly involved C. Or it would be through following his suspicions of D that he would come on the trail of E. At all events it was all very exciting and provocative and he would settle down to a busy stay in the town.

He found the Queen Victoria hotel near the station and it conformed well to John Moore's description 'old-fashioned commercial'. Its grey façade, square and ugly, promised large rooms and high ceilings and great golden letters ran across it proclaiming it to be 'family and commercial'. The proprietor, whose name was Rugley, lived with his wife on the premises and had done so for more than thirty years. He saw no reason to make changes in the hotel which had always given him a comfortable living and he was deaf to talk of what a gold mine it would be if he would instal central heating and strip lighting, knock down a number of walls, build a modern kitchen, engage a skilled cook, and put television in every bedroom.

"When we first came here," he told Carolus, "it was just the same, only in those days they wanted me to put in an American cocktail bar and have the radio in all the bedrooms. They were only fashions, gone out years ago, same as their fads today will go. We keep on as we've always done except that I put running water in the bedrooms before the war to save the girls running round with jugs of hot water. Otherwise we don't change. I hope you'll be comfortable."

When Carolus looked round his large heavily curtained bedroom with its mighty mahogany bed and worn Axminster carpet, he was content. It must have been in rooms like this that he and many of his generation were born and he felt as though he were returning home. His room was number 3, he noticed before he came down to the bar.

This was crowded with men, mostly middle-aged business types.

"It's the Rotary today," explained the barmaid who served him, a short brisk woman known as Doris. "We get them once a month. They'll all be going in for lunch in a minute."

She said this in a confidential tone as though she thought Carolus was eagerly waiting for a chance to converse with her, and when, as she predicted, 'the Rotary' trooped out she leaned over the bar.

"I saw you were booking in," she said. "I thought to myself, well that's a funny thing, the last gentleman we had come here on his own was the poor fellow who was murdered. You've read all about that, I suppose."

"Yes. I've read something of it."

"We had him in here, you know," went on Doris proudly. "Yes, he stayed all the evening drinking doubles. Didn't he, Vivienne?"

"Mmmm," said Vivienne.

"He wasn't drunk, mind you. We wouldn't have served him if he had of been. But he wasn't sober, either. You should have seen the way he walked out of here. As though he was holding on to a rail, he went. Then no sooner had he got down to the shelter than this murderer knocked him on the head with a coal-hammer. It doesn't bear thinking about, does it?"

"Yes," said Carolus. "Had you ever seen him before?"

"Me? Him? Never in my life. I said to Vivienne— didn't I, Vivienne?—I've never seen *him* before. It wasn't a face you'd forget, either. Staring eyes, he had, like I don't know what. Seemed to drill right into you. And he was talking all this about having been presumed dead and coming back to life though some wouldn't like it. Enough to give you the creeps. Which room have you got?"

"Number three."

"I thought so. That's the room he had, only Mr Rugley doesn't like it being talked about. You don't need to worry because it's all been done out since. The police came and took away what little he had and it's been cleaned nicely. It's nothing to upset you now."

"It doesn't," said Carolus. "After all, he wasn't murdered there, was he?"

"Oh, what a thing to say! Of course he wasn't. I'm surprised at you saying a thing like that. D'you hear what he says, Vivienne? He says, 'he wasn't murdered there, was he?'"

"Mmmm," said Viviennne with a remote demure smile.

"Thank goodness he wasn't," went on Doris. "We've had enough of it as it is with the police here every five minutes asking questions. I told them the last time, I said, perhaps you think one of us done it? They didn't like that. Well, it's silly, I think. If they can't find out who it was, what's the good of asking me what time he went to the telephone? I said to them, what do you think I am? An alarm clock? I can't tell you what time it was. It was after seven, I do know that."

"You're not really sure whether he did telephone, I suppose?"

"He went in the box all right because George saw him. That's the porter. Whether he got through or not I don't know. Only it seems funny if he didn't, otherwise who was to know he was going to that shelter? It's not everyone would go there on a night like that with an icy wind nearly cutting you in half every time you looked out."

"So you think he arranged to meet the murderer there?"

"That's what it looks like, doesn't it? Though who's to say now? I don't suppose we'll ever know the truth about it. It's a funny business all round. Of course, it quite upset me'n Vivienne at the time. Well, it would, wouldn't it? Anybody being murdered like that. But I don't think much more about it. One of the papers was going to put my picture in, only it never came to anything. Still, it's an experience. All in a life, as you might say."

"Did this man seem nervous?"

"No, it wasn't that. He didn't seem as though he was expecting it to happen, if that's what you mean. He kept filling up with another double Scotch till I wondered where it would stop, but you couldn't say he was jumpy or afraid of anything. He didn't take much notice of the other customers, either. I was surprised, really, when I heard about it after. Well, it wasn't what you'd expect, was it? But I said at once to Vivienne that there was something very funny about him. Those eyes! I shall never forget them. And the way he talked about coming to life again. We both thought it was funny, didn't we, Vivienne?"

"Mmmm," said Vivienne whose glance was fixed on faraway things in the ceiling.

"It's not every day you get anything like that," Doris went on. "I sometimes wonder what it will be next."

"I suppose," Carolus said, as though it was of no great

concern to him but he wished to make conversation, "I suppose you didn't notice whether any of your other customers had their eyes on him at all?"

"It's funny you should ask that," said Doris. "Because I said to Vivienne afterwards, I said, Mr Lobbin seemed quite taken up with that fellow, I said. He could scarcely take his eyes off him. He's ever such a nice man, Mr Lobbin. Has the paper shop a few doors away. I've never heard him say an unkind word. What it was about this other fellow I don't know but he stood there watching him for a long while."

"Did he say anything to you about him?"

"Yes. Asked me his name. And when George had looked it up in the book I told him, but he didn't make any remark."

"Anyone else interested?"

"Not that I was aware of. This fellow didn't do anything to call attention to himself, really. There may have been others who noticed him. I couldn't say. But Mr Lobbin certainly did."

"No one followed him out? Rafter, I mean?"

"You want to know a lot, don't you?" said Doris good-humouredly.

"Yes, I do," said Carolus at once, deciding that frankness with Doris would pay. "I've been employed to investigate this murder."

"Detective, you mean?"

"An interested party."

Doris nodded. "I see. Well it *is* interesting when anything like that's happened. No, I don't think anyone followed him out, particularly. Only I noticed Mr and Mrs Bullamy, who were sitting over there, went out soon after. I noticed it because they never go before closing-time. I said to Mr Bullamy, are you going? I said, and he said, yes, he said, we've got to feed the baby. He was only joking, because they've got no children. They're only staying in the town, not residents, but they come in every night, regular as clockwork, and stay till we close. You ought to see her! She's quite a nice party but she looks more than half like a man. He's smaller than she is. They've got a little money, I should say, though they don't throw it about. You'll see them tonight if you're here."

" Where are they staying? "

" Oh right up the other end of the town."

" When did Lobbin leave the bar that evening? "

" Oh, not till we were just going to close at ten o'clock. That's about usual for him. You see his wife has all the say. He seems scared of her though he's a big fellow. It's a shame, really. She's one of those that never stop. Nag, nag, nag. He's a quiet peaceable sort of man. That very evening he was telling me they'd had a real up-and-downer and he'd come out to get away from it for a few minutes. I said I didn't wonder. I know what she is. A proper tartar. Still, there you are. It takes all sorts to make a world, doesn't it? "

" I gather the murdered man's family lives in Selby. Do you know any of them? "

" Only by sight, really. I'd never heard of them before this happened. Vivienne knows Mrs Dalbinney, don't you, Vivienne? "

" Mmmm," Vivienne assented and added, " she lives in the block of flats where my husband works."

After that somewhat surprising confession her attention went back to the distances.

" Yes," enlarged Doris, " Vivienne's husband is the night porter at Prince Albert Mansions, so they're both on at night, which suits them very nicely. This Mrs Dalbinney has a big flat on the first floor, very posh Vivienne says it is. She's Separated, you see. When I heard she was the sister of this fellow who'd been murdered I couldn't help laughing. It seemed funny because he was half down-and-out-looking, as you might say, and from what Vivienne says she's very high and mighty. Oh, very high and mighty she is, Vivienne says. Her sister's not, though. That's the unmarried one, Miss Emma Rafter. She's started coming in here—Vivienne serves her, don't you Vivienne? There's nothing stuck-up about her. It's more horses and that. She looks that sort, too. Always with a big Boxer dog."

"What about the brother, Bertrand Rafter?"

"I don't know anything about him. They say he's very quiet. He never comes in here. Well, if it's true what they say he can't very well. See, he's living with that young secretary of his. I don't know why they don't get married. They've been together a long time, now. I tell you who does come in sometimes, though. That's young Dalbinney. He can't be more than twenty-one or so and they say he's ever so clever. Has a lot to say for himself, anyway. Books and that."

"He wasn't here on the evening we're talking about, was he?"

"I wonder. I can't be sure, really. I don't think he was, else I'd have remembered. Unless that was him talking to Mr Stringer over there. No, that was another night. I'm sure he wasn't in, was he, Vivienne? Young Dalbinney? On the night that fellow was murdered?"

"I really couldn't say," said Vivienne without much feeling.

"I don't think so, anyway," said Doris, dismissing the matter. "Are you going to have lunch in the hotel? They've got sheeps' hearts on today."

"I might," said Carolus, thinking this was the end of Doris's confidences, at any rate for the moment.

"You'll enjoy them. Our cook does them ever so nicely. And I'll try and think of anything else I can tell you. Oh! There was one thing I didn't like. When he first came in—this fellow who was murdered, I mean—while he was sober he paid with a note pulled from his pocket case. A small case it was, the folding kind, that he took from his hip pocket. But when he'd had a few of those large whiskies he pulled out an envelope full of money and paid from that. It looked like a lot of money to me and I didn't like it, with him having had a lot to drink."

"Did you say anything?"

" No. It wasn't for me to say anything. I didn't think any more about it, really."

" Have you told anyone else this? "

" No. I've only just remembered it. And the way those police spoke to anyone I shouldn't have told them whatever happened."

" An envelope? "

" Yes. Just an ordinary envelope. He kept it up in his breast pocket. I think there was some writing on it."

" Did anyone else see it? "

" I don't think they could have done. Not here, anyway. There was no one near him at the time."

" Did you know everyone who came to the bar that night? "

" Pretty well. I didn't know who Miss Rafter was at the time, but I heard after. There was no one out of the ordinary in that evening."

It was three weeks since the murder, yet Carolus felt very close to it. The splendid little Doris could obviously think about nothing else and had been remarkably observant. Then Carolus was occupying the room in which Rafter was to have slept and drinking in the bar in which he had spent his last evening. This afternoon, moreover, Carolus intended to walk down to the shelter on the promenade in which the body was found. That time had passed since the murder was unimportant. Carolus felt, as he had intended to feel, in the thick of it.

More so when after lunch he set out for a walk along the promenade. There was a direct road called Carter Street from the Queen Victoria hotel to the sea as he had noticed when he had driven over it this morning. Carolus took it and reached what he took to have been the point at which Rafter was hesitating when the policeman saw him. Nothing whatever could be deduced from that hesitation. He could have been merely wondering, in a half-drunken stupor, whether to turn left or right, or he could have been debating in which direction the last shelter lay if he had made an appointment to meet someone there. Or just getting his breath.

54

At all events he had turned right and Carolus did the same. There had been a strong wind against Rafter, he remembered, and very few people about. Today there was a last streak of pale sunlight on the sea and it was cold. He passed a number of people well wrapped up who seemed to be taking their exercise seriously.

Ahead of him he counted four shelters, about two hundred yards apart, so that the last was nearly half a mile away. It would have taken Rafter at least ten minutes, in that wind, to reach it. The first two shelters were fairly well occupied but, by the time he reached the third, people passed less frequently, and in the shelter only two people sat looking rather chilly.

Beyond it no one seemed to be walking. The road dividing the promenade from the houses which overlooked the sea now curved inland, leaving a long triangular garden between it and the promenade. This garden broadened out till by the time Carolus reached the last shelter he was thirty yards or so from the road. The garden had iron railings and before approaching the shelter Carolus turned in to it and spoke to a man working there.

"Is this garden l. ked at night?" he asked.

"How many more times?" asked the man. "If I've been asked that question once I've been asked it a score of times since this murder's happened. Yes, I lock it myself every evening at eight in winter and ten in summer. Never do to leave it open. You'd be surprised what they get up to if a garden's open at night."

"No I shouldn't," said Carolus truthfully. "It was locked on the night this man was killed?"

"Certainly it was. That's not to say someone couldn't have popped over the iron railings if he was a bit nippy. It's been done before. We had a lot of plants stolen last year."

"You've no reason to think anyone did so that night?"

"No, I haven't. The police was examining all along the railings and in the flower-beds and that. I don't know whether they found anything. They don't say. But I saw

no sign of it having been got into. If this murderer was
the sort of Jack the Ripper I think he was . . ."

"Surely you're thinking of Spring-heeled Jack?"

"Yes, that's what I meant to say. It wouldn't have been
much trouble to him to nip over."

It would not, thought Carolus, and, again not approaching the shelter, he crossed to the railings on the other
side, below which was the beach.

Here, too there would be no difficulty. The pebbles
were perhaps four feet below the level of the promenade
and anyone, even a determined woman or elderly man,
could have made that descent, then crept along under the
promenade wall till he wished to climb up again. But
why? It was dark and the murderer was, presumably,
alone. Why not walk openly back?

At last he came to the shelter itself. He did not know
exactly where the murdered man had been found and
it did not matter. It was the situation of the shelter which
interested him rather than its interior. Quite alone,
nearly a hundred yards from a house, beyond the usual
limits of pedestrians' passage even in daylight and almost
certain to be deserted on a dark windy night, it was the
ideal place for a carefully planned murder. Retreat from
it afterwards was easy.

There was something eerie about it, here in the fading
light with the sea roaring grimly not many yards away
and the harsh scream of sea-gulls audible. Whoever had
chosen this place had imagination of a macabre sort and
a taste for the dramatic.

Carolus stood gazing at the shelter and the beginnings
of a notion came to him.

7

SINCE Carolus had been 'called in' by Mrs Dalbinney
he decided to see her that afternoon. He found Prince
Albert Mansions easily enough, a mighty piece of

masonry occupying one side of an open square. He went up to the first floor and found Mrs Dalbinney wearing something that he believed was called an 'afternoon frock' or a 'tea gown'. Her sustained gentility rather irritated him. He longed to say something vulgar. But he held his tea-cup and nodded gravely while she talked.

"Actually, Mr Deene, we do not feel that your intervention is necessary now in view of the exorbitant fees you mentioned. The whole unpleasant matter seems to be evaporating."

"Evaporating?"

"The police have asked us no further questions and the unfortunate gossip in the town has subsided. We begin to think that it may be better to let sleeping dogs lie."

"Your late brother Ernest being the sleeping dog, I take it?"

Mrs Dalbinney looked rather haughty.

"I was speaking figuratively," she said. "I meant that this very disagreeable incident will soon be forgotten."

"You don't want to know who killed your brother?"

"You seem anxious to stress the relationship. We wish to forget it."

"I don't think that will be possible until the murderer has been discovered and tried. At all events you have asked me to investigate and I intend to do so. So let's start with your own movements on the night of the crime."

Mrs Dalbinney flushed.

"I find that remark in extremely poor taste," she said. "I have already given the police any such information as they require."

"Then you won't mind repeating it to me. I understand you went to the cinema with your sister?"

It did not seem to occur to Mrs Dalbinney to wonder what was the source of this information.

"What could be more pointless than a recital of my movements on that evening, Mr Deene? You are in search of a murderer, I think? Perhaps you suggest that *I* was walking about with a coal-hammer and that *I* attacked my brother with it? "

" I have formed no opinions at all. But I do seriously recommend you to answer my question. If I am to accomplish anything for the fees you are going to disburse I must know these details."

Mrs Dalbinney seemed to struggle with herself for a moment.

" It's *too* ridiculous," she said at last. " I haven't the least objection to the whole world knowing, but . . . Oh very well. I went to the pictures with my sister Emma."

" At what time? "

" We met at seven-thirty."

" Where? "

" In the foyer of the Palatine Cinema."

" That is on the front, I think? "

" It overlooks the sea, yes."

" You go often? "

" *De temps en temps*. I find television tiresome and vulgar."

" But not the cinema? What film did you see? "

" Actually, something rather macabre. *The Black Island*. There was a shorter film with it. Perhaps you would like to know that we came out at ten o'clock and returned here. . . ."

" Immediately? "

" I beg your pardon? "

" Did you come straight here from the cinema, Mrs Dalbinney? "

Mrs Dalbinney rose.

" No, Mr Deene," she said in a satirically dramatic fashion. " No, I first marched along the promenade with a coal-hammer in my hand and murdered my brother with it! Are you satisfied with that? "

" No, I'm not. I'd like to know if you came straight here."

" Of course I did. Now please don't be ridiculous. I have never walked along the promenade at night in my life."

"Did anyone see you return?"

"My sister came with me."

"No one else?"

"I really have not the slightest idea."

"Was your son in when you returned?"

"He was not up. Whether or not he was in bed I cannot say. I do not invigilate my son's movements."

"No. Of course not. You did not go out again that night?"

"Out? Certainly not. My sister stayed here for the night. She frequently does so."

"There's a question I must ask you and everyone else even remotely connected with the case. Have you ever had in your house a heavy hammer like the one used by the murderer?"

"Really, Mr Deene, I cannot be expected to know what tools may or may not be about the house. I have certainly never noticed such a thing."

Carolus seemed to consider for a moment, then brought out a very different question.

"Do you know a man named Lobbin?" he asked.

Mrs Dalbinney's manner changed.

"Why do you ask me that?"

"I just wondered," said Carolus. This was perfectly true. He wanted to prolong his catechism because he felt the woman was not being frank, and had hit on this name as the first local one that occurred to him.

"Has someone been gossiping maliciously?"

"I don't know. What do you know of Lobbin?"

Mrs Dalbinney looked uncomfortable.

"Mr Deene," she said. "I have found your questions silly and impertinent but I believe you have some pretensions to being a gentleman. If you have been told anything relating to myself and the Lobbins I trust you will treat it with the contempt it deserves."

"I will when I know the truth of the matter. What is it?"

"I will give you my confidence. Lobbin's wife is a most offensive woman. Most offensive. Some months ago there

59

was an incident of a very humiliating kind. I would prefer to forget it but since you have apparently heard something of it you had better know the truth."

"I should like to."

"Lobbin himself is a harmless individual, clumsy, tactless and of course without the instincts of a gentleman. But he meant no harm. He asked me if he might call on me to give me some information which he thought would interest me. I gave him permission to do so and one evening at six o'clock he came here. Most unfortunately, as it happened, no one was with me. It is impossible to find domestic servants now and I have only a daily woman. I was alone here.

"Lobbin, of course, behaved with complete propriety, gave me his information and went away. But under the stress of the nagging of his wife he apparently revealed to her that he had made this call and she, either from stupidity or design, put a most monstrous interpretation on it. She arrived here on the following evening and demanded to see me. My daily woman, who fortunately stayed late that day, with the greatest courage told her I was out but she forced her way into this room and began to say the most unspeakable things."

"Such as?"

"I should not dream of repeating them. Had I wished to make it a police court action she would have been heavily fined or sent to prison, but of course I could do nothing of the sort. She actually suggested that there had been something improper between her husband and me."

Carolus succeeded in suppressing a smile.

"Really!" he said.

"It would not be the first time, she shouted in coarse and ringing tones, that she had discovered her husband's infidelities. Can you imagine anything so sordid? And this was supposed to relate to *me*! To me, Mr Deene. I was too angry to speak. Eventually my daily woman, who showed the greatest resource, ran down and fetched the night porter."

"Vivienne's husband," said Carolus.

" I beg your pardon? "

" Nothing. I'm sorry to interrupt."

" The night porter, a large and serious-minded man, was able to remove the woman from this apartment and I gave orders that she should never again be admitted, even to the hall downstairs."

" You haven't been troubled again? "

" Not directly. But I gather that this woman's venomous tongue has continued to spread the vilest slanders. I have consulted my brother Locksley Rafter, who is a solicitor. He came to see me about it quite recently. Actually, on the afternoon of the day on which this wretched man was found murdered."

" I see. Now what I should like to know, Mrs Dalbinney, was the nature of the information Lobbin brought to you that day."

" Why? What possible relevance can that have? "

" Difficult to say. But I should like to hear it."

Mrs Dalbinney paused.

" You may not believe me, Mr Deene, but I must tell you that this is the first time I have realized that it *may* have some relevance, for it concerned my brother Ernest, whom I then believed to be dead."

" Indeed? "

" Yes. It appeared that Lobbin had been a prisoner of war with him and they had undergone forced labour together on the notorious Burma Road. He remembered my brother well. The name ' Rafter ' is an unusual one. The family goes back to Plantagenet times when a certain Simon de Rafter or de Raefter . . ."

" Yes, yes. Very interesting. Didn't Lobbin at once recognize the name when he heard it? "

" He did not connect it. He would naturally not associate a man such as he had known with the members of my family."

" I see."

" But someone eventually told him that we had lost a brother in the East during the war and he decided to tell me what he remembered of him."

61

" And what did he remember? "

" It is an old story, Mr Deene, and a disgraceful one. I suppose every family like ours with a long record of public service and a distinguished name has some skeleton in the cupboard and I'm sorry to say my brother Ernest was ours. What Lobbin told me only confirmed what I already knew. My brother Ernest betrayed his fellow-prisoners to the Japanese. He was a collaborator."

" It must have been dreadful for you to learn that," said Carolus sincerely.

" It was indeed, particularly for my brothers, who both distinguished themselves in the war; Bertrand in the CMP became a Provost Marshal and Locksley was in the Judge Advocate's department. But we knew about Ernest fifteen years ago and had had time to forget it. One black sheep in such a flock is understandable."

" And Lobbin confirmed it? "

" Eventually, yes. He started by trying as it were to gild the pill but I told him frankly that we were aware of my brother's treachery, on which he told me an extraordinary story. Ernest, it must be understood, spoke some Japanese. Before the war he had gone to Tokyo to represent his firm and had picked up a fair knowledge of the language. From the moment of his capture he showed himself willing to give the Japanese any information he had. This might not have been so serious since as a mere NCO he could not, perhaps, give them much very valuable information. But it went further than that. He was put among other prisoners for the very purpose of spying on them and reporting their movements to the enemy. This went on for a considerable time until his fellow prisoners became suspicious. They watched him and were convinced that he was a source of information to their captors. When they had sufficient proof of this, they decided to kill him.

" Ernest was always a crafty creature and a sneak, even when we were children. He was able to forestall the men who wanted to kill him. He persuaded the Japanese to give out that he had been shot. The sound of a firing-squad was actually simulated, I believe. In fact, he was moved to another camp under another name.

"But Lobbin was unaware of this. He told me first that my brother had been shot by the Japanese for refusing to betray his comrades. When he heard that I already knew some of the truth he said that he and his comrades had the gravest doubts as to whether Ernest had been shot at all. I thanked him for his information and that was the end of the matter."

"Was this the first time that you had heard your brother's death doubted?"

Mrs Dalbinney hesitated.

"He was reported Missing Believed Killed," she said. "Afterwards, in connection with my father's estate, he was presumed dead."

"But you, Mrs Dalbinney, what did you think?"

"I *believed* him dead. But of course there always was an element of doubt. Not sufficient to embarrass us in connection with my father's estate, but still a trifle disturbing on an occasion such as I describe."

"Did you tell your brothers and sister what you had learned from Lobbin?"

"Certainly. We are a very united family. We talked the matter over at length. It was pointed out by my brother Locksley that even if there was any truth in this story of Ernest's survival, it need not perturb us now, for Ernest might only have postponed his fate and even if he was still living was unlikely to admit his identity."

"So that his brothers and sisters could remain in possession of his part of the estate?"

"You must understand, Mr Deene, that it was not the money we thought about but the scandal and distress which his return would bring to us. My brother Locksley considered it quite likely that Ernest would be publicly disgraced, if not tried and sentenced for his treachery. In a family like ours that would be hard to bear."

"In any family," said Carolus quietly. "So you were all a bit jittery about it?"

"We were, for a time, a mite uneasy. But as my brother

Bertrand said, the situation had existed since 1944 so there was no reason to suppose it would come to anything now."

"You had no further indication that Ernest was alive? "

"None whatever until the body of the murdered man was identified as his."

"Who identified it? "

"There was a great deal of external evidence and my brothers were able to give more. There is no doubt about it. The body was Ernest's."

"Suppose he had not been murdered. What do you think your family would have done in the circumstances, Mrs Dalbinney? "

"We have never discussed it. I think, for my own part, that a financial adjustment would have been made, provided Ernest continued to live abroad under a different name."

"Very sensible."

"It would have avoided the scandal. That is our main concern. That is why I came to see you, Mr Deene. I need scarcely say that we had no other apprehension in this matter."

"But when you came to see me the scandal had already broken. It was known that the murdered man was your brother."

"We wished it to be cleared up as quickly as possible. As soon as the murderer was found and tried the whole wretched thing would begin to fade out of the memory of the public. I have my young sons to think of. I do not wish them to grow up with a shadow of this kind over them. And now tell me, Mr Deene, have you begun to form any ideas on the subject? "

"No. I only came here this morning. I find it a most baffling and intriguing mystery."

"Intriguing? That sounds very flippant when our family name is at stake."

"Not really. I am never flippant about murder. Indeed I am told I am inclined to be pompous about it. But in this case I do not feel that the victim need be greatly mourned. That does not make me any less anxious to identify his murderer. Even if it was an act of revenge."

"Revenge? You mean Ernest may have been killed by someone who suffered, all those years ago, from his treachery?"

"It would be a motive, wouldn't it? One must always consider who can have a motive for murder."

Mrs Dalbinney grew somewhat excited.

"I see! You think he may have been recognized . . . Mr Deene! Do you realize that there was someone in Selby that night who *had* suffered from his treachery? Who *had* once planned to murder him? Who *would* have recognized him?"

"You are going altogether too fast. If you mean Lobbin, we don't know that he was among those who are supposed to have planned to murder Ernest Rafter in a prison camp. We don't know that he recognized him."

"But it's remarkable! I begin to see . . ."

"Please let me warn you, Mrs Dalbinney, against any such hasty ideas. I only said that I should be no less anxious to find the murderer even if his motive was revenge. There might be many reasons for revenge. There is a great deal of Ernest's life about which we know little or nothing. And revenge, anyway, is only one of a number of possible motives."

"Still, I feel convinced that you are seeking in the right direction. Pray continue with your investigations, Mr Deene, and forget that I expressed any doubt about the necessity for them. You are an extremely percipient man. I do not think the police themselves are aware of this link with Lobbin."

"If they are, they are scarcely likely to regard it as a link. Certainly not as a motive for murder."

"We shall see!" said Mrs Dalbinney.

8

DORIS received him like an old friend when he went into the bar of the Queen Victoria that evening.

"You know what we were talking about, don't you?" she said leaning across the counter confidentially. "Well that's one of that lot over there by the mantelpiece with the Boxer dog. Emma Rafter, that is, and she's taken to slipping in for a couple of quick ones since all this happened. Worried her, I daresay. She's mad on horses, so they tell me, and I told Vivienne just now, she's rather like a horse herself. Didn't I, Vivienne?"

"Mmmm," said Vivienne, loftily amused.

"She's a very good soul, I believe, but she does look a bit of a freak, doesn't she? She's always got that Boxer dog with her."

Not really a freak, thought Carolus. In a way she looked rather handsome, though he could see no likeness to her sister. The 'horsiness' referred to by Doris was not a crude and mannish quality. One could see it, yet one would imagine her riding side-saddle. She was quite alone and Carolus went across and introduced himself. She was polite enough but seemed nervous.

"Oh yes. Isobel told me. You're going to find out everything for us."

"And *about* you," said Carolus facetiously. "May I get you a drink?"

"About us? Oh thanks. Yes, gin and tonic."

Vivienne served Carolus and when he returned he found Emma Rafter looking even less at ease.

"I hope you clear it up. It's been dreadful. For me, particularly."

"Why for you particularly?"

"Because Ernest . . . you see, he and I were much of an age. We were together a lot as children. I never believed all that was said about him. He was rather a selfish boy, I know, and not very straight, but I was fond of him and when this happened . . . I mean, it *was* my brother."

So there was one person at least who expressed some kind of regret at Ernest's death.

" Your sister seems chiefly concerned about the scandal it has caused."

" Oh, she's like that. She does not mean to be heartless but she does rather worry about family, and she has the two boys to think of. That side of it means very little to me. In fact I think my business has improved since this happened."

" I didn't know you had a business, Miss Rafter."

" Yes. Out at Purshott. The only bit of hunting country left around here. I've got stables."

" I see. I envy you."

" Do you hunt? "

" Only murderers," said Carolus. " I never seem to have time for any other kind."

"Shame. Do come out if you feel like it. Meet my partner. I'm out there every day."

" Did you go out there on the day of the murder? "

" I wonder why you ask that. Yes, I expect I did. Can't remember now."

Carolus caught Doris's eye. She seemed to have something to say to him and when, a few minutes later, Emma turned to speak to a friend he went up to the counter.

" I forgot to tell you," she said, her lips almost touching his ear as she leaned across. " She was in here that night. The one you're talking to, I mean. She only came in for a minute Early On. I remember by the dog. I believe it was the first time she'd been in here."

" Was the man here then? "

" I couldn't say. You don't really notice anything like that, do you? "

"Yes," said Carolus. " At all events you would have noticed if they'd recognized one another and spoken, wouldn't you? "

" Ten to one I should have unless I was busy at the time."

Carolus returned to stand beside Emma Rafter.

"I'm sorry if I seem to ask impertinent questions," he said. "Perhaps it's because I've got so little to work on. You see, the only people known to me or, I think, the police, who can be thought to have the shadow of a motive for this crime are the members of your family. It may seem to you, as it seems to your sister, 'ridiculous', but it means that I must start by asking you all a few questions."

"It doesn't seem to me ridiculous," said Emma. "I can quite see the point of it. What do you want to know?"

"When did you last see your . . . brother, Miss Rafter?"

"Ernest? Nearly twenty years ago."

"You had no reason to think he was still alive?"

"Isobel had some story from a man who had been a fellow-prisoner of his, but I didn't take much notice of it."

"But since that story? Nearer the time of his death?"

"See him, you mean?"

"Yes. Or hear that he was alive?"

"Even if I had believed that story Isobel heard I should certainly not have believed he would come to Selby."

"Would you have recognized him if you had seen him, do you think?"

"I doubt it. My brothers went to the mortuary to identify him, but of course he was dreadfully disfigured. . . ."

"I meant if you had seen him alive."

"I don't know. How can I know that?"

"Only, in fact, if you *did* see him alive. Did you, Miss Rafter?"

Carolus watched her keenly.

"I wondered when that question would come," she answered after a pause. "I know that I must have been in this bar at the same time as he was because I came in for a drink on my way to meet my sister and I have since

68

been told what his movements were. But I have not been asked till now. Perhaps it did not occur to the police that I might have come here. The answer is—no. I was here for about five minutes only. I did not observe who was in the bar. I saw no strangers. If my brother Ernest was here I did not recognize him or even notice anyone who might have been him. So I can't help you there."

"It seems strange that having come to England with the idea of revealing himself and, one would suppose, claiming the money left to him in your father's will . . ."

"How do you know that's what he came for?"

"I don't *know*. But I do know he went to Somerset House to examine the will. And he would scarcely have come down to Selby unless he intended to see his family."

"Then why didn't he get in touch with his family at once?"

"It is not known whether he did or not. He had six hours here. He certainly went to the hall from this bar with the idea of telephoning."

"You think we're lying, then?"

"Miss Rafter, I must keep an absolutely open mind. But I repeat that it seems strange that neither during the two weeks of his stay in London nor during the six hours of his presence in Selby did he, apparently, communicate with any of you."

"I see your point. But we don't lie, Mr Deene. You haven't met my brothers yet?"

"No."

"When you do so you will have a better understanding of them. They are both incapable of that kind of deceit. The first they knew of Ernest for nearly twenty years was that he had been murdered in a shelter on the promenade. Except for that story Isobel heard."

"May I ask you one or two more questions?"

"Yes. Of course."

"Let's go back to the day of the murder. You are not sure whether you went out to your stables at Purshott?"

"I expect I did. I can easily check on that if it's important. I know I came here at about seven o'clock."

"And stayed only five minutes? Yet you were not meeting your sister till seven-thirty, I believe?"

Emma Rafter seemed more impatient than worried by this question.

"I did not count the minutes. Mr Deene. I say I came here about seven—it may have been five or even ten past. I stayed about five minutes—it may have been seven or even ten. I then had ten minutes walk to the Palatine. I don't know whether we met at precisely seven-thirty. It may have been seven-twenty-five or seven-thirty-five. And so on. But when I left here I went straight to the cinema."

"You did not make a phone call?"

"No."

"Or go into the hall of this hotel?"

"No."

"The film was?"

"*The Black Island.*"

"What time did you come out?"

"Again I don't know to the minute but somewhere about ten."

"You were both on foot?"

"Yes.'

"And walked straight back to Mrs Dalbinney's flat?"

"Virtually, yes."

"You mean?"

"This is too silly. I've told Isobel she's absurd. In fact we crossed the road to the promenade for a moment to get the stale air of the cinema out of our lungs. She asked me to omit this from my statement to the police because she thought it might involve us in some way as witnesses."

"Why? Did you see anything or anyone?"

"Yes. We saw the man who had told Isobel that story about Ernest. A newsagent called Lobbin."

"Oh, you saw Lobbin."

"He crossed the road in front of us, coming from the town. It did not seem important to me but Isobel asked me not to mention it."

"How long were you on the promenade?"

"I should say at the most two minutes."

"Who suggested going across? "

"No one. It was a custom of ours. We often go to that cinema together and usually go and sniff the ozone before retiring."

"Your sister told me very indignantly that she had never walked along the promenade at night in her life."

"That's true. We don't walk along it. We cross it, go to the rails and return." She was smiling now. "Is it very reprehensible? "

"You remained together that evening? I mean, after you left the cinema you were not apart for a moment? "

"Not till we went to bed at about midnight."

"You didn't see Paul Dalbinney? "

This seemed to startle Emma somewhat.

"Paul? No."

"He had gone to bed? "

"I don't know. Probably. There's nothing much to do in Selby after the cinema."

"One last question. Did either of you make or receive a phone call after returning to Mrs Dalbinney's flat that evening? "

"One last answer. No. Now you have a drink with me."

When Emma Rafter had gone Carolus went across to the counter where Doris and Vivienne were unoccupied for a few moments.

"The first rush is over," explained Doris. "We usually get them in soon after we open till now, when it Goes Quiet. Then we're busy around nine. Did you find out what you wanted? "

"Yes," said Carolus.

"She's a scream, really, isn't she? But not a bad sort when you get to know her."

Carolus, who was sure about neither of these, nodded.

"I wish you could remember whether she was here at the same time as the man who was murdered that night."

"It's no good my making it up," said Doris, "and I can't be sure either way. I know she was in Early On that night and so was he, but whether it was the same time or not I can't say. Did you notice, Vivienne? "

"What was that?" asked Vivienne.

"Whether that fellow with the staring eyes was here at the same time as Miss Rafter that night?"

"I couldn't say, I'm sure," replied Vivienne from far away.

"Only Mr Deene wants to know. He's trying to find out about the murder. I tell him I can't be sure. It must have been about the same time, mustn't it?"

"Mmmm," said Vivienne without interest.

"I could ask Mr Lobbin when he comes in. He might have noticed. He was here all that evening as I told you."

"No. Don't do that," said Carolus. "I'll be having a chat with him later and can ask him myself. But I'd like to know which he is, if he comes in."

"Oh he'll be in all right. He's usually in before this. It's the only bit of peace he gets all day to come in here. She's on at him like I don't know what from the time he gets up in the morning. Such a nice fellow, too. Wouldn't hurt a fly. Still, they're the ones that marry them, aren't they?"

"Are you married?" asked Carolus.

"Me? Gracious no. You won't catch me marrying any-one. No thank you. Vivienne is, though, aren't you, Vivienne?"

"Mmmm," said Vivienne without enthusiasm.

"Is there anyone else you want pointing out to you?" Doris asked Carolus.

"Do you ever get a man called Bodger in here?"

Doris smiled.

"Hear that, Vivienne? No, we don't. He used to come in a lot until a few months ago but we don't have him in here now. Well, I told Mr Rugley I wouldn't serve him again. Mr Rugley was quite all right about it. 'I don't blame you', he said. Well, I mean to say."

"What did he do?"

"It wasn't so much what he did but the things he said. I told him, that last time he was in; 'Don't you come in here again, I said, else you won't be served'. He's really a terrible old man. You should have heard

72

the way he spoke to Vivienne, didn't he, Vivienne? "

" Mmmm," admitted Vivienne.

" Ever so rude, he was. I should have liked Vivienne's husband to have heard him, that's all. But then he's like that with everyone, I believe. I know they won't have him in the Chequers now."

" I believe he lost his only son in the war."

" That's no excuse," said Doris with unaccustomed severity. " There's lots did that and still know how to keep a civil tongue in their head. Besides it's a good many years ago now."

" Still," said Vivienne melodiously, " they say that's what turned him."

" I don't know what turned him, I'm sure. Someone did tell me he thought the world of his boy and the two was always together in his boat and that. But I can't see why we have to put up with his language all these years later. So long as he doesn't come in here."

Carolus invited them to have a drink.

" Mmmm," said Vivienne, adding graciously, " I don't mind. Plain gin."

" Well, that's very kind of you," said Doris cheerfully. " I'll have a small gin and french same as I always do. Scotch for you? Yes, that old Bodger. He'll get into trouble one of these days."

" I hear he has been in trouble."

" Oh, that. I meant the way he speaks to anyone." Suddenly she leaned across to Carolus. " This is Mr Lobbin coming in now," she whispered. " Yes, it is a cold night," she added loudly to Carolus. Then to the new-comer, " Good evening Mr Lobbin. Cold out? "

" It *is* cold," said Lobbin.

Carolus studied him. He was six foot tall or a little more and his face had a rough untidy look about it, a wayward moustache, disorderly eyebrows and irregular features. His eyes had a hurt, wondering expression and his hands were large and powerful. Yes, Carolus could well believe he was nagged by his wife, though there might be a dangerous limit somewhere to his patience.

Carolus decided not to speak to him this evening or until he had made more progress with Rafter's own family. But he watched him go at once into an intimate conference with Doris which lasted several minutes before it was broken up by Doris's loud, "So that was it? Well, I'm not surprised really."

Lobbin was, Carolus grudgingly supposed, the nearest he had so far to a 'suspect', yet on the face of it he could not take the supposition very seriously. True, Lobbin had known Ernest on the Burma Road, knew of his treachery and had perhaps suffered from it. True, he had seen him in this bar on the night of the murder, as Doris said 'could scarcely take his eyes off him' and so probably recognized him. True he was on the promenade shortly before the murder. But to argue from these that he had gone down there, found Rafter and murdered him, seemed to Carolus far-fetched. Besides, what about the coal-hammer? Did he customarily walk about with a coal-hammer concealed on his person in case he should meet a man who had behaved badly as a fellow-prisoner of war nearly twenty years earlier? There had not been much time, one would think, between Lobbin's leaving the Queen Victoria at ten o'clock and his being seen near the Palatine Cinema also at 'about ten o'clock'. At all events there had scarcely been time for him to walk to his home, provide himself with the coal-hammer, and reach the promenade.

The more Carolus thought about it, the more it seemed to him that all his vague suppositions were misdirected. The Rafter family, the people recognized by the policeman on the promenade, were all he had at present to consider as suspects but he could not make himself take their so-called motive seriously.

When a few minutes later a man and woman entered the bar, whom he recognized at once from Moore's description as Mr and Mrs Bullamy, he felt even more that he was among improbabilities. Mr Bullamy was a jolly little man and his wife looked like a female impersonator. Mr Bullamy made a joke with Doris and his wife laughed whole-heartedly at it. They both drank Guinness and seemed to enjoy it. What in the world could there be to connect such a commonplace couple with a brutal and cowardly crime except that by chance they had walked along the promenade on a night which was, admittedly, one of blustering wind, shortly before a man was murdered there?

He noticed, however, that they greeted Lobbin at once and the three sat down together. Mr Bullamy ceased to joke and chuckle and listened gravely to something Lobbin was explaining. Mrs Bullamy became rather tense. But then, Carolus reflected, they had all three recently been questioned by the police and had in common the anxiety and disquiet which such questioning might rouse in even the most innocent persons.

On the whole he felt he had done enough for today. Tomorrow he would start from quite a different angle and leave both the family and this pub for a time while he saw one or two even less involved people whose names had been connected with the thing. But he knew he was floundering about in the dark.

9

NEXT morning Carolus went by appointment to call on the Reverend Theo Morsell at the Vicarage of St Giles's. He found this to be a stucco villa on the outskirts of the town.

Mr Morsell was a vigorous-looking man in his early forties whose hair was thinning fast and whose eyes had a hungry look, as though they were spying out occasions for exercising his bounding energies. He had an embarrassingly warm and boisterous manner, called Carolus 'old man' or 'old chap' and seemed accustomed to being popular, uncontradicted and admired.

It very soon became apparent that, so far from thinking that Carolus had approached him as someone who might be considered a suspect, he assumed that he was being consulted for his sagacity and experience.

"I'm a bit of a sleuth myself," he said in a hearty way as he lit a large pipe. "Always interested in this sort of problem. In my job I have to know something about human nature at its best and sometimes at its worst. So I've made a bit of a study of crime and criminals. It has enabled me to lend a hand here and there, too. I'm delighted to say that at least five of my regular congregation have done time and two of my choir are ex-Borstal boys. Grand fellows, all of them. Grand. So I'm not exactly a novice. May be able to help you quite a bit, old man. You tell me where you've got to and I'll see whether light breaks."

Carolus inwardly squirmed but remained civil and businesslike.

"I've got to that night on the promenade," he said, "and I understand that you . . ."

"Ah, that night," said Mr Morsell. "Now the first thing we should notice about it was that there was a blustering cold wind. Not at all a night on which people would be walking up and down the promenade by chance."

"Yet you . . ."

"The second thing was the *time*. Just after closing-time, you notice. Just when anyone who wanted to cool his head might take a blow."

"Is that why you . . ."

"But the key to the whole thing as I see it is the coal-hammer. If we could find where that coal-hammer came from, we should be well on the way to the murderer."

"Obvi . . ."

"Unless he'd been clever enough to steal it to involve someone else. If I were you I should go all out on discovering a home from which a coal-hammer is missing. The police should go about it systematically and try every door in Selby. Someone must have noticed it by now. If you hear of one missing it would narrow down your suspects to those who have had a chance to steal it, wouldn't it?"

Carolus gave up, for the moment, any attempt to ask relevant questions.

"You think it was pre-planned, then?"

"My dear old chap, of course it was. And with a cunning given to few. The murderer was no sadist, but someone with a very good reason for wishing this man dead. If he had been a paranoiac there would have been an element of sexual perversity in the crime, whereas it was a shrewd and clever thing, a triumph of mind over matter which he thought would remain immune from discovery."

"What was the motive, then?" asked Carolus.

Mr Morsell shrugged.

"Revenge," he suggested, "greed, fear, pride, it could have been any of the usual motives. No power on earth would make me believe there was not a valid reason. There was too much logic and skilled reasoning in the affair."

"That almost means you suspect one of the family."

"My dear man, I suspect no one yet. I am much too old a hand at this sort of thing to fix on anyone. All I can say is, this looks to me like a cold-blooded affair and not the act of a sadist or exhibitionist. So a motive has got to be found. That's where you come in, you field detectives, accustomed to dealing with these things in a practical way."

Carolus made a resolute attempt to put his first question.

"I understand you were on the promenade that evening."

"I was indeed," said Mr Morsell. "But unfortunately I saw nothing which could be at all helpful to you. A pity, because my powers of observation are unusually keen and if there had been some little incident or encounter which would give you any scope for enquiry I should have noted it in detail. But there wasn't."

"Perhaps you will let me decide that," said Carolus, driven towards exasperation at last. "What time did you go down to the promenade?"

"My dear old boy, I'm hopeless at remembering times.

77

As my wife will tell you, she has to remind me of every
appointment. It's a congenital weakness of mine. But I
should guess that in this case we left here soon after nine
o'clock. We dine about eight. When I say 'dine' I mean
we have our evening snack. That night we sat for some
time over it before deciding to face the elements. I may
say we didn't realize, quite, what a disagreeable night it
was. The wind must have come up in the late afternoon.
Yes, we can call it nine o'clock, or soon after."

"How long were you down there?"

"There again, you've come to the wrong shop for
detail. We drove down from here, parked the car by the
pier and set off with that wind in our faces. I should
think we walked for about fifteen minutes before turning round."

"How far did you get?"

"Not unfortunately, as far as the last shelter or we
might have seen something useful. But I can tell you
the point we reached to an inch. We went as far as the
public lavatory. I know that because I intended to make
use of it but found it closed."

"So what did you do?"

"My dear old chap, I don't know whether you suffer
from a weak bladder. If you do you will guess what I
did—got over the railing and dropped on to the beach
for a moment out of the light."

"So your wife was waiting alone on the promenade?
Did anyone pass her?"

"You must ask her that for yourself. She'll be bringing
us in a cup of coffee in a moment. We always indulge
ourselves at eleven o'clock in the morning. You'll join
us, I hope? I know how exhausting this kind of teaser
can be."

"Thank you. So that was as far as you went?"

"Yes. Pity, isn't it? If we had covered the next hundred
yards or two it would have brought us to the last shelter,
and then who knows what my observant eye might have
seen?"

"Who indeed? The man was being murdered about

78

the time you were on the beach," said Carolus, but again apparently failed to suggest to Mr Morsell that this was anything but a consultation with a fellow expert.

"How absurd! To think that I might . . ."

"You turned back immediately?"

"As soon as I rejoined my wife, yes. It was good to get the wind behind us."

"Did you meet anyone during the whole of your walk?"

"I can't be too certain about this because we go down to the promenade about three evenings a week. I remember that as we were walking against the wind we were caught up by a very short fat man who was stepping out briskly in the same direction. So briskly that he was soon out of sight ahead of us. And I seem to remember meeting a policeman at some point. I have an impression that there may have been one or two others but I can't be sure."

"You did not speak to anyone?"

"Only to a parishioner," said Mr Morsell as though certain that this could have no bearing.

"Who was that?"

"My dear old boy, I can't see that it can have the remotest connection with your problem. It was a parishioner of mine."

"So you said. It was the name I wanted."

Mr Morsell laughed.

"You sleuths!" he said. "You must find a few wrong trees to bark up, I suppose. What noses you have for red herrings! Here was a man who sings bass in my choir, born and bred in Selby, who has worked in the same ironmonger's shop for twenty years, and who chanced to take a stroll that evening. Yet you want his name. But I like you for it, old chap. I like thoroughness even when it's misplaced."

"Thank you. What was his name?"

"Oh really!" said Mr Morsell, a touch of irritation coming into his manner. "Aren't you going rather far?

I don't want my friend upset by a lot of questions when he cannot possibly be concerned."

"You decline to tell me whom you met that evening, Mr Morsell?"

"I'm sorry, old fellow, but I don't think you have much sense of humour. If you could see the person concerned! " Mr Morsell laughed. "Oh dear! " he added chuckling.

"Did you tell the police about this?" asked Carolus, whose face had not changed.

"The police? My dear old boy, what do you take me for? Do you think I want to make such an ass of myself? The police would have told me not to be ridiculous."

"I see. Then since you refuse to tell me I shall have to inform them that you know of someone on the promenade whose name you do not wish to give."

"Hoity toity! " said Mr Morsell. "Now you're becoming very public-spirited. I respect your sentiments but I wish you could see how absurd the whole thing is. The man's name was Stringer. But please, my dear old chap, don't go after him with a deerstalker. He's a good, quiet little man, fond of reading and devoted to his wife and children."

"Thank you," said Carolus again.

"What we have to think of is not these diversions, surely, but the real murderer, who must be splitting his sides by this time to see you and the police barking up every tree but the right one. He certainly seems to have had either extraordinary intelligence or extraordinary luck."

"Exactly," said Carolus. "One of the two."

"Or both," went on Mr Morsell. "Unless you find out from whence that hammer is missing I don't see him ever being discovered."

At that moment, as the clergyman had predicted, his wife entered with a tray. She was a gloomy-looking woman, heavy and with cheeks of a dull yellowish texture. She produced a grudging smile for Carolus.

"Beryl, my dear," said Mr Morsell while his wife was

pouring coffee, " Mr Deene has been asking me all sorts of searching questions about the night of the murder. I've told him that I had to leave you for a few moments. . . ."

" When? " asked Mrs Morsell blankly.

" You remember. During our walk. When we found the public convenience locked."

" Oh yes. I told you it would be."

" So you did," said Mr Morsell brightly, " and I didn't believe you. But not for the first time I was wrong and you were right. You remember I went down on the beach for a few moments? "

The ' few moments ' were a trifle stressed, Carolus thought.

" Yes," said Mrs Morsell.

" Mr Deene wants to know if anyone passed you."

" I don't think so," said Beryl Morsell dully.

" How long were you waiting, Mrs Morsell? "

" It seemed a long time," she sighed.

Mr Morsell laughed.

" I expect it did. All on your own in that wind! " he said.

" How long? " asked Carolus.

" It seemed hours," said Mrs Morsell.

" You see? " said her husband delightedly. " She's even worse about time than I am. It was about three minutes, wasn't it, Beryl? "

" I suppose so."

" That's what you sleuths are up against," laughed Mr Morsell. " Three minutes become ' hours ' if you don't nail your informants down. And did *no* one pass you? "

" There may have been. I don't remember anyone. I was cold."

" Oh dear, oh dear! If all your witnesses were as vague as that, where would you be, eh, Deene? It's a good thing I know what kind of information you require."

" Do you often go out on the promenade at night? " asked Carolus, unmoved by the clergyman's complacent flippancy.

"Quite often, yes. We both benefit from sea air. I've said many times, there's no point in living here if we don't take advantage of it."

"Always at the same time?"

"No, no. It varies widely. Sometimes we go just after tea. Never later than we were that evening. Whenever we can fit it in."

"Had you seen the people you encountered that night on previous occasions?"

"Yes. The policeman certainly, and I think the little muffled-up man. Yes, I'm sure of it."

"What about Stringer?"

"Forever Stringer, eh?" chuckled Mr Morsell. "I happened to mention to Mr Deene that we saw poor Stringer that evening, my dear, and he has seized on it!"

"Did we?" asked Mrs Morsell rather vacantly. "I don't remember."

"Yes, you do. Just when we were about to go back to the car."

"I don't remember."

"Do you remember anyone else, Mrs Morsell?"

"You don't, do you, dear?"

"Wasn't there a policeman?"

"Apart from him," said Carolus.

"I don't think so," said Mrs Morsell.

"What time would you say it was when you reached your car?"

"Getting on for ten, I should think," said Morsell.

"Don't you remember?" his wife asked. "I told you we should miss the News. It was ten o'clock."

"So it was! This time my wife's better than I am."

Carolus finished the coffee in his cup and stood up.

"If you feel like a yarn at any time, old boy," said Mr Morsell, "don't be afraid to look me up. Two brains are better than one, you know. We'll argue it out together. I can always find time for crime."

"Thank you," said Carolus, "I think you have told me all I want to know about your movements. Oh by the way, do you use a coal-hammer?"

Mr Morsell gave his jolly laugh.

"I'm sorry I doubted your sense of humour," he said.

"Do you?" persisted Carolus.

"Not for lethal purposes, old chap. Whether we have one in the coal shed I couldn't say."

Mrs Morsell, pleased by her feat of memory over the time when the News was missed said—"Don't you remember buying it, Theo? From Taunton's. Mr Stringer served you. It must be about a year ago."

"Did I? Well, well. I daresay I did, though I can't for the life of me remember it."

"Do you use it?"

"Do I, my dear?"

"Of course you do, Theo. For those big lumps."

"Oh, *is* that the thing we're talking about? That sledge-hammer sort of thing?"

"It is pretty heavy," his wife agreed.

"I wonder if I might see it?" asked Carolus. "I've been hearing so much about coal-hammers, I should really like to see what one is like."

"Certainly, dear old boy," said Mr Morsell, and disappeared to return a few moments later with a heavy hammer grimed with coal.

"I wonder what you used before you bought this," said Carolus, examining it.

"I don't think we used anything," said Mr Morsell quickly.

"I seem to remember another, once," said his wife. "But it was lost ages ago. It wasn't quite as heavy as this if it was the one I mean."

"Have you seen the actual weapon that was used?" asked Morsell of Carolus with an air of professional interest.

"No. I can't say I have," Carolus replied. "The police don't put it on show."

"Pity, I think. Someone might recognize it."

Carolus was now in the narrow entrance passage.

"Who's next on your list?" said Morsell.

"I rather want to see a man called Bodger."

"Old Bodger!" Morsell smiled. "Yes, I daresay you do want to see him, the old villain. I should think that anyone investigating a crime in Selby would start with old Bodger."

"Would you? But I've started with you."

"So you have, and I do hope my comments have been some use to you. I know our lamented Detective Inspector Burton often tackled Bodger, and not in vain. 'If old Bodger knows nothing about it', he used to say, 'there's nothing to know.'"

"Where does Bodger live?" asked Carolus.

"I can give you his address in a moment, old chap."

"Parishioner of yours?"

"Hardly. He's not what they call round here a church-goer."

"But you know him?"

"Who doesn't? As a matter of fact we had him here the other day to do a small job for us. He used to be a ship's carpenter, you know. He's a very handy fellow when he likes. He built me a whole shed outside, beside the coal shed."

"How long ago would that be?"

"Three or four months, I daresay."

"He was seen on the promenade that night."

"There!" said Mrs Morsell with uncharacteristic animation. "What did I tell you?"

"My wife is always ready to think the worst of Bodger," said Mr Morsell. "I must say he was extraordinarily rude to her last time he was here."

"No! Not that, Theo. Only I said . . ."

"You said you'd never have him in the house again and I don't blame you. Now, this address. Let's see—ah, here it is. 19 Archer Street. That's in what they call the Old Town. One of those narrow streets. I believe the old boy lives alone now. His daughter used to look after him but she got married."

Suddenly there was a startling surprise from Mrs Morsell.

"Poor girl," she said and gave a queer throaty laugh.

10

FROM all he had heard of Bodger, Carolus supposed that this would be one of the toughest contacts to make and he debated with himself how to go about it. Should he find out what pub Bodger used and lie in wait for him there? Or should he go straight to his home and chance being turned away? On the whole he decided that though it was a gamble he would try the second of these.

He realized as soon as he faced the old man that it was touch and go. Bodger, tall and powerful, though in his seventies, stood on the brick floor of his tiny cottage looking down at Carolus in the narrow roadway. A smell of cooking came from behind him and Bodger looked impatient as though he had just left his stove and wanted to go back to it. He was clean-shaven with silver-white hair and he wore a navy blue jersey.

"What do you want?" he said.

"I wanted to ask you about something," said Carolus, with deliberate feebleness.

"Ask away," said Bodger without moving.

"I can't very well, in the street," Carolus said.

"What's it about?"

"It's about that man who was murdered."

"I can tell you all I know of him," said Bodger, "and I don't need to go behind closed doors to do it. He deserved all he got and if I had known who he was I'd have done it myself. Does that satisfy you?"

"I don't say I don't agree with you, but . . ."

"Were you in this last war?" asked Bodger.

"Yes."

"Army?"

"Yes."

" Burma? "

" Yes."

" Come inside. Sit there. Why should you bother to find out who was the killer when you know very well what kind of man it was he killed? "

" I'm more concerned with who wasn't the killer," said Carolus. " Somebody will be charged sooner or later and it might as well be the right one."

" You a policeman? "

" No."

" Then what's it to do with you? "

" Curiosity," said Carolus. " I want to find out the truth about it. I'm interested."

Bodger grunted.

" You speak straight, anyway," he said. " Why have you come to see me? "

" You were on the promenade that night and you had reason to hate the murdered man."

" Not personal reason, I hadn't. I mean, not this particular man. And anyway I didn't know anything about him. I didn't even see him. But if you want to ask me questions you can. I wouldn't talk to the flaming police. Just wait while I go and take something off the stove."

While the old man was out of sight Carolus looked about him. It was a small brick-floored room whose door opened on the street and whose little window was almost hidden by flowerpots in which grew geraniums—not, Carolus noted, of the common varieties. There was no fire in the grate but it was laid ready. Apart from that the whole room reminded him of a small ship's cabin, everything in it being neat and clean and carefully in place. The old man might live alone, Carolus thought, but he certainly knew how to look after himself. Moreover there was something about Bodger and his surroundings which suggested that he had more culture and knowledge than might be supposed and his manner of speaking was that of a man of some education. Carolus saw on the mantelpiece a photograph of a rather handsome youth in uniform. It was signed ' Dad from Danny 1940 '. Carolus realized that he had been invited to take a chair with its back to this.

Bodger returned.

"I don't know what you want to ask," he said, and sat down opposite Carolus with a table between them.

"Nor do I, quite," admitted Carolus. "I'm foxed by this case. A man has the top of his head smashed in by a coal-hammer in a lonely shelter on a windswept promenade at ten or ten-thirty at night. I know the place, the time and the weapon. I know a few people in the vicinity at the time. Beyond that I know very little. The murder was pre-planned yet I know no one who could have foreseen that the victim would be there."

Bodger nodded.

"You come to me because I was one of those down there that night?"

"Yes. And because I have been told how you would feel about a collaborator of the Japanese."

"I see. Well, I was down there that night and I do feel like that about any bastard who collaborated. What's more, I've got what's called a bad name in this town. So perhaps you'd better start by supposing I did it. How's that?"

"Suits me," said Carolus. "Do you often go down to the promenade?"

"Never, if I can help it. Only to get down to my boat in the summer. Do I look the sort that would go walking up and down there?"

"Frankly, no."

"I don't know why I did that night. I'd had a bit of a row with the landlord of the Chequers."

"What about?"

"Something he said I didn't like. I told him what I thought of him, drank up and walked out. You can find plenty to tell you of similar things I've done in the town if you like to look for them. I don't get on much with people."

"Nor do I. So you came out of the Chequers?"

" I don't know what made me go across towards the sea. I'd had one or two but I wasn't drunk by a long way. I wanted to hear the sea, I think."

" To hear it? "

" Yes. I like the sound of the sea, especially on a rough night. It's a sound I'm used to. I don't have any flaming radio or television or that. Don't like 'em. Lot of talk and I don't go much on music either. But I can listen to the sea for hours. It's never twice the same, you see. I can think, when I hear the sea. Seems to set my mind at rest. Rough and blustering or quiet and gentle, it's all the same to me. I just listen for a bit and I'm right as rain. I don't suppose there are many feel like that, but there it is. That's why I went across that night, I daresay, though I wasn't to know it at the time. I just thought I'd take a walk before coming home for a bit of a read."

Carolus glanced at a couple of shelves of well-used books.

" You read a lot? "

" Not extra. I like a read now and again. War books and that."

" Did you notice anyone else on the promenade? "

" Flaming copper."

" You knew him? "

" Me know a copper? I wouldn't demean myself. I wouldn't know one from another though there isn't one of them that wouldn't swear they knew anyone if it suited them. I saw this bastard's uniform, that's all."

" Anyone else? "

" I didn't take note of anyone. I daresay there were others about. I was thinking."

" What time did you come home? "

" It was late," said Bodger sourly. " I sat in a shelter for a time. Not that last one. Right up the other end, away from that, as it happened. Must have been getting on for eleven when I came back here."

" You don't remember seeing a short stout man well wrapped up? "

"No. I don't. I don't remember seeing anyone except one couple I know. They come from Australia."

"Like the murdered man," reflected Carolus.

"Is that where the bastard had been since the war? I didn't know."

"What is the name of the couple you met?"

"Oh, they had nothing to do with it. Don't start thinking that. They're harmless as they can be."

"Still just for the record I'd like their name."

"Bullamy, it is. They're staying at Pier View, a bit of a boarding house on the front by the jetty."

"Yes, I've heard about them and seen them. Did you stop to talk with them that evening?"

"No. To tell you the truth I'm not one for talking much. I don't know what's made me tell you as much as I have."

"You haven't explained what you said when I first came to the door. 'If I had known who he was I'd have done it myself.'"

"So I would have. I think you know why."

"I've got an idea."

"What would you feel about a collaborator if you'd lost your son on the Burma Road? Twenty-one he was when he died. Just had time to do his training and out there to be taken prisoner in his first few weeks. He was my crew on the old boat before the war. Just him and me ran it together. Decent living it gave us then. Good life it was, until the war came along. I always knew there *were* people who worked with those flaming Japs, getting a bit of extra food for giving their mates away, but I'd never met one. If I had, there's no telling what I'd have done."

"This man Rafter was a notorious collaborator. It was known in the town that the Rafter family had a brother with that reputation."

"I heard that," said Bodger. "I'd have told them what I thought about it if it would have done any good. But it wasn't their fault, I suppose."

"So you knew about Ernest Rafter?"

"I knew there had been such a person though I didn't know his name. He was supposed to be dead, I thought."

"You had no reason to think he was still alive?"

"I never thought about it."

"Still less that he had been in London for a fortnight?"

"How should I have known that?"

"I don't know. But you can see that it looks somewhat odd that on the one night when you decide to take a walk on the promenade a man of whose treason you had heard, a man you had particular reason to hate, was murdered in a lonely shelter there."

"Yes. I see what you mean. I told you you'd better start by suspecting me. But I don't see how you're ever going to get further than suspicion."

"I may not, but the police may. They have expert means of turning a suspect into a certainty, from finger-prints to a thread of cloth."

Bodger's face changed not at all.

"I'm not worried," he said somewhat enigmatically and Carolus rose to go.

He walked back to the car, which was some distance away, for in the maze of narrow streets, some of them cobbled, among which was Bodger's cottage, there was no room for him to drive.

Back at his hotel he went to the bar. The clock above the heads of Doris and Vivienne showed twelve-thirty and Carolus enquired about lunch.

"It's a nice piece of silverside today," said Doris, " with dumplings and carrots. Jam roll to follow. Cook told me as I came in. But you don't want to go to the dining-room before one o'clock, because they're having *their* lunch then and don't like it if they have to hurry. Well, no one does, do they? We have ours when we close. How are you getting on with your detection? "

"Nicely, thank you," said Carolus, amused.

"I tell you who's coming in this morning, or at least so they said last night, that's Mistr' an Mrs Bullamy. You know, those two who you saw. Yes, they said they'd be in this morning. 'We've got to do a bit of shopping', they said, 'so we'll just pop in for one before lunch'. To tell you the truth it's Not Much where they're staying. They like to get out when they can. Don't they, Vivienne? "

"Mmmm," said Vivienne, effectively expressing her entire indifference to the question.

"You can't blame them, really," went on Doris, who was not easily damped. "Specially when they're on holiday. I think it's upset them being mixed up in this murder, too. Well, it would anyone, wouldn't it? The police questioning them and that. They don't say a lot about it but you can tell. Anyway, I should have a talk to them if I was you. You never know what they may be able to tell you."

When Mr and Mrs Bullamy came in Carolus found that it was easy enough to get into conversation with them, and that they were quite willing to talk about the murder, alternating chattily.

" I'd like to know what they think we can have had to do with it," said Mr Bullamy with a suggestion of aggrievement.

"We're just staying here for a holiday," chimed in his wife. "We'd never heard of the man in our lives. I can't think what they want to ask us about it for."

"I expect they just wanted to know whether you had seen anything that would help them," said Carolus.

"We told them we hadn't. I wish now we'd never come to the place."

" I certainly wish we hadn't decided to go for a walk along the front that night. That's what did it, you see, us being down there not far from the shelter. Silly, though, isn't it, when they must know very well we had nothing to do with it? "

"Do you think we shall be called up as witnesses? "

" It depends on what you saw," said Carolus.

" There was nothing, really. Only this little fat man all wrapped up in scarves."

" You didn't see Lobbin while you were down there? "

"No. We didn't see Mr Lobbin. And if we had we shouldn't have thought anything about it. He's a very nice fellow, Mr Lobbin, and no more to do with any murder than the man in the moon."

"You saw no one in fact but the policeman and the small man with the scarves?"

"Well . . ." said one.

"Not on the parade we didn't," said the other.

Carolus waited.

"There was this man crossing the road," said Mr Bullamy.

"I shouldn't think he was anything to do with it," said his wife.

"I never mentioned it to the police because, to tell the truth, it slipped my memory and I don't suppose it's so important I need go running round there taking up their time and mine with something that may have been nothing at all."

"Crossing the road?" said Carolus.

"Yes. We thought of it next day when we heard what had happened. Otherwise it would never have occurred to us to think twice about it."

"It was only by chance we remembered it then, really. I said to my husband, do you remember seeing that man crossing just by the Gents' convenience, I said, and he remembered it, too. Only we never would have otherwise."

"Yes that's how we came to remember it."

"What?" pressed Carolus patiently.

"This man. You see there weren't many about that night. . . ."

Carolus sighed. Not many? 'That time of darkness was as bright and busy as the day.' And now here was another, apparently, to increase the roll of promenaders.

"More than seems quite natural on such a dirty night," said Carolus, but this was not answered.

"As I say, we'd just got as far as the Gents, and were thinking of turning back when we saw this man crossing the road."

"Near you?"

"No. A little way ahead. It must have been just about by the last shelter."

"But there is no road there. A garden begins before that and the road curves away from the sea."

This seemed to baffle Mr Bullamy a moment but he soon recovered.

"I know," he said. "This was *before* the road curved. Must have been, mustn't it? You couldn't judge just where anything was in that light. Anyhow, we saw him."

"Crossing towards the sea?"

"No. No, no. Away from it," said Mr Bullamy impatiently, implying that any fool would know that.

"You mean, you had the impression that he had come from that shelter and was returning to the town?"

"I suppose that was it, though of course there's no telling."

"But, Mr Bullamy, as you state the matter you must have been quite near this man. From the urinal to the point where the road curves away from the promenade is only a few yards. Can you tell me what he looked like?"

"Oh just an ordinary man. Medium height I should say. . . ."

"A little more than medium," suggested his wife.

"What was he wearing?"

"A grey overcoat. That's all I saw."

"More browny-grey," said Mrs Bullamy.

"Light-coloured, anyway. What about his face?"

"It was an ordinary sort of face. Nothing out of the way."

"Age?"

"You couldn't tell. Forty perhaps. . . ."

"More like fifty," said Mrs Bullamy.

"Clean-shaven?"

"I think so."

"Hadn't he got a little moustache?" wondered Mrs Bullamy.

" I should have said clean-shaven."

" Did he give the impression of being smart or shabby? "

" I'd have said fairly smart," said Mr Bullamy.

" I thought rather on the shabby side," his wife argued.

Carolus took a deep breath.

" Would you know him again? "

" Oh yes! " said Mr Bullamy.

" I'm quite sure I should! " agreed Mrs Bullamy.

" You had never seen him before? "

They agreed that they hadn't.

" Or since? "

" No," they chorused.

" But you would know him if you saw him? "

They were certain of this. After a small inward struggle Carolus asked them if they were sure they had not told the police of this and when they said 'no' lectured them on the unwisdom and even danger of holding back information. He then resumed his own questioning.

" You're sure it was a man, not a woman? "

" Oh yes. I saw him clearly enough for that."

" Hurrying? "

" Yes. He was stepping out pretty smartly."

" You didn't notice what he did when he had crossed the road? "

" No. I can't say I did. You seem very interested."

" I am. I'm trying to find out the truth about this murder."

" Sort of detective, as you might say? "

" Sort of."

" So that's it. Well, we don't want to get mixed up in it more than we can help. But we don't mind telling you anything we noticed if it would help."

" You came here that evening? "

" Yes. We dropped in. We do most evenings. There's not much to do where we're staying."

" Did you see the man who was afterwards murdered? "

" Not to take any special notice of. When it all came

out afterwards we knew it must have been him with those staring eyes, but not at the time."

" He didn't speak to you? "

" No. I don't think he spoke to anyone except Doris. Not while we were here, anyway."

" You had never seen him before? "

" Not that we were aware of. You never know with people, do you? "

" Yes," said Carolus. " He was apparently a striking-looking man."

" I daresay. We didn't notice."

" You usually stay until closing time? "

" Very often we do."

" But that night you left a few minutes after half past nine."

This brought a flow of alternating explanations from Mr and Mrs Bullamy.

" To tell you the truth we're not over-fond of that Vivienne," said Mrs Bullamy in a low voice. " She thinks too much of herself. We got quite sick of it that evening."

" It was stifling hot in here," said Mr Bullamy. " We felt like a blow before we went back for the night."

" They don't like us out late, where we're staying. It means them stopping up, you see, and they're early birds."

" I think I must have eaten something that didn't agree with me that evening. I was feeling a bit off from the time we came in here."

" You don't want always to stop to the very last minute, do you? It looks so bad."

" This place was crowded that evening. There was nowhere to sit down. My corns were giving me a bad time, too."

" You hadn't noticed this man leave the bar? " asked Carolus.

" No. We weren't paying any attention to him, really."

" Thank you for telling me all you have," said Carolus,

as though they had made important revelations. " By the way, where do you normally live, Mr Bullamy? "

This caused an awkward check in the flow of confidences.

" I've not long retired," said Mr Bullamy.

" We don't really live anywhere," explained his wife.

" We're waiting to find somewhere to settle down, really."

" We're thinking of staying here."

" But where did you live when you were working? "

" Well, I was born in Croydon," said Mrs Bullamy quickly.

" I'm a Cheshire man," added Mr Bullamy.

" You worked in London, perhaps? "

" I did for a long time, yes. I lived Brixton way then."

" Some time ago? "

" Yes, it is."

" Where have you been living since? " persisted Carolus, trying to sound chatty.

" I don't quite see what it's got to do with it. We were in Brighton before coming here."

Carolus brought things to a head sharply.

" You were in Australia, I think? "

There was a long and difficult silence, after which Mr Bullamy said—" Whoever told you that? "

Carolus followed his successful attack.

" Did you know Ernest Rafter out there? "

The Bullamys had better defences now. Mr Bullamy smiled broadly.

" Always the same," he said. " You people in England talk of Australia as though it was a small town in which everyone knew everyone else. It's a continent, really."

" There are nine million people in Australia," said Mrs Bullamy.

" Did you happen to know this man? "

" Not that we know of," said Mr Bullamy.

" He used a different name, we've been told, so how are we to know? "

" It would be too much of a coincidence, wouldn't it? "
suggested Mr Bullamy.

" No," said Carolus and without referring to the
matter again took their glasses to the counter to be re-
filled.

" There! " said Doris confidentially leaning close.
" Whatever have you said to them? They look as though
they'd seen a ghost! "

" Perhaps they have," replied Carolus.

I I

THAT evening Carolus decided to retrace the footsteps
of the murdered man as far as he could from the time of
his arrival in Selby. He had not done such a thing in any
previous case but he was so much at a loss here that he
clutched at anything which might stir his imagination.
His previous visit to the shelter had been made soon
after his arrival, this would be made at the same time as
Ernest Rafter's. Indeed this afternoon and evening he
would try to see and hear things as the murdered man had
done.

Reaching the station at half past five Carolus waited
till the 4.15 from London got in on time at 5.40 and
joined the passengers from it as they came out of the
station. Most of them went to the car park, the taxi rank
or the bus stop and he found himself almost alone
in the rather gloomy road which led to the Queen
Victoria.

But he met one pedestrian who came towards him from
the direction of the hotel with a Boxer dog.

" Good evening, Mr Deene," said Emma Rafter.

" Good evening. Having an evening stroll? " suggested
Carolus chattily.

To his surprise she stopped. She seemed to think it
necessary to explain her presence.

" I live just up there," she said. " A small flat in the

block at the top of the road. I'm going to get my evening paper."

" From our friend Mr Lobbin? "

" From his shop. Yes."

" Perhaps I shall see you later? We might have a drink if you're coming to the Queen Victoria."

" I daresay I shall—for a few minutes."

It was just five to six when Carolus entered the hotel and noticed Doris on her way to open the bar. In the office was Mr Rugley the proprietor, a pleasant elderly man with whom Carolus had chatted on several occasions.

" I didn't know you'd come here to make enquiries about the murder," he said to Carolus, not severely, but with just a suggestion of reproach.

" Yes. Curiosity as much as anything, I'm afraid."

" Finding out all you want? "

" No. Very little. It's a tough case. By the way, did Rafter book in under his own name? "

" Yes. I didn't even notice it at the time. You don't, you know, and it wasn't very clear writing."

" Could I see the entry? "

" The police took my book the very next day. I've had to get a new one. The whole thing's been a nuisance, Mr Deene. I wish I'd never let him a room."

" Did he have much luggage? "

" No. Only a little case. The police took that as well. He didn't pay for his room, of course, and when she heard about it Miss Rafter wanted to pay but I said no. It was no responsibility of hers."

" Was there anyone staying in the hotel at the time? "

" No visitors. Just the wife and I and George the porter. He's been with us a good many years."

" Rafter said nothing to you except that he wanted a room? '

" No. Just the usual things. He thought he'd be staying about a week."

" Then he went up to his room? "

" For about half an hour. I saw him come down and make straight for the bar. Then I went to our sitting-room to watch the television. I never saw him again, though the girls in the bar did of course."

" And George."

" I believe George did see him for a minute in the hall. He comes on at seven, so you can ask him."

" Thanks, Mr Rugley."

" That's all right. I hope you find out who did it. It doesn't look as though the police will. They've been on it all these weeks. Only I didn't know you were here to investigate."

Carolus went up to his room, the room to which Rafter had gone at the same time. He had half an hour to pass and wondered what his predecessor had done in that interval. A wash, perhaps, a moment's unpacking of his single case, then what? He drank heavily when he reached the bar so what can have kept him from it here? There was no telephone and the only heat came from a shilling-in-the-slot electric stove. Was he writing a letter, perhaps? Entering up a diary? Going over notes or instructions? Or just looking at the evening paper? It seemed unlikely to Carolus that he would ever know.

At half past six he went down to the bar and since Doris was occupied in a whispered conversation with Mr Lobbin was served by Vivienne. He took his whisky and stood near the door to notice later that he was being discussed by the two behind the bar—or rather, discussed by Doris and disdainfully scrutinized by Vivienne.

Presently he crossed to them and asked for the telephone.

" There! " said Doris. " You gave me quite a start. That's just how he came up and asked for it on The Night. I told him to go into the hall and phone."

" Is that all you said? "

" No. Now I come to think of it I asked him if it was a local call he wanted to make, because he might need the change for the box. I'd quite forgotten about that till now."

" What did he say? "

" He seemed to think for a minute then said it was. I

99

told him I could give him the coppers but he took no notice and went straight into the hall."

" How long was he out of the room? "

" I couldn't say, really. It was while he was out Miss Rafter came in. But George may know. He was in the hall at the time."

" I'll ask him," said Carolus, glad of an excuse to follow Rafter's movements without making it obvious that he was doing so.

But he had a surprise. As he entered the hall from the bar he nearly collided with Emma Rafter.

" Always come in this way," she explained, and might have added, Carolus thought, that this discreet route to the bar was followed in deference to her sister's gentility.

George was foxy and fiftyish, a leathery old type in the ostler tradition. He said " Evening, sir," to Carolus and only just failed to touch a forelock.

" I wanted to ask you one or two things about the night on which Rafter was murdered," said Carolus and noticed that George nodded with understanding, evidently prepared for this. " You were here in the hall when he came from the bar to telephone? "

" Yes, sir. I was."

" Was anyone else? "

" How d'you mean? "

" In the hall, I mean. Did he happen to meet anyone but you? "

George looked dull and crafty.

" Not that I noticed," he said.

" And you *would* have noticed if he had? "

" I daresay I should."

" He didn't, for instance, meet Miss Rafter, as I did just now? "

George became emphatic.

" No, certainly not, he didn't. I'm quite sure of that. No, he never met Miss Rafter. That I could swear to."

" Did she come through this way that evening? "

" If she did I never noticed it."

This could be the truth, thought Carolus, or the result of a small bribe.

"Rafter asked for the telephone box?"

"Yes, and I showed him."

"He telephoned?"

"That I can't say. He went into the box and was there some time. But it's sound-proof and I couldn't tell if he got through."

"He was some time in there?"

"Seemed like it. I didn't notice particularly."

"Did you know his name at the time?"

"No. No one did, that I know of. You couldn't read much of his signature. It looked like Rapper to me when I just looked at it. Later on Doris asked me to look at the name and I saw it was Ernest Rafter."

"Did that mean anything to you?"

"Not at the time it didn't."

"Thank you, George." Carolus tipped him. "If you happen to remember anything you might let me know."

"I will, sir. Certainly sir."

Carolus went into the phone box and examined the local directory. There were five entries under 'Rafter', two for Emma, her flat and her stables out at Puckshott, two for Locksley, his home at Bawdon and the office of Rafter and Mohawk, Solicitors, at Bawdon, and one for Bertrand, his house in Selby. Under Dalbinney was 'Mrs Isobel de L'Epée Dalbinney'. It seemed unlikely that if Rafter had wished to speak with one of his relatives that evening he had not been able to do so.

It was just 7.15 when Carolus returned to the bar and found Emma Rafter on the point of leaving. He tried to delay her but she seemed in a hurry now. He wondered if she was going to the pictures with Isobel but made no enquiry.

He now had to pass the long period during which Rafter had been knocking back a series of double Scotches and he realized that this would be nearly two hours. So far as he knew the only person with whom Rafter had talked during that time was Doris, but several others had been present, including Lobbin, Stringer and the Bullamys. Lobbin was here now and Carolus thought that more than once the newsagent eyed him curiously and remembered that he 'could scarcely take his eyes off' Rafter.

Presently he noticed that Lobbin left the bar without saying good-night to anyone. Carolus had the impression that this was neither a final departure nor a moment's absence. He approached the end of the counter at which Doris was standing and leaned towards her, a signal to which Doris responded so heartily that their heads almost touched.

"You remember the night of the murder?" asked Carolus unnecessarily.

"Shall I ever forget it?" whispered Doris, wide-eyed.

"Do you remember whether Mr Lobbin stayed in the bar continuously that night? Or whether he went out at all?"

"Well, I never thought to mention it when the police were on to me, but I know he did slip home for a minute some time in the evening because when he came back he told me about it. He was worried about Her, you see, and went round to see what was happening, but she went for him like a vixen. Hammer and tongs it was again till he had to leave her and come back here for peace and quiet."

"Thank you," said Carolus. "Who is the man who has just come in?"

"That's Mr Stringer," said Doris, then, drawing herself up, dismissed Carolus with a loud "It only shows, doesn't it?" before turning to greet the newcomer and pour out a light ale for him.

Stringer was a lean and narrow little man, almost entirely bald, who wore old-fashioned gold-rimmed spectacles. He immediately went into conference with Doris, and Carolus turned his attention to the Bullamys who had just come in. They said good evening to him rather hurriedly before being served by Vivienne.

At nine o'clock or a few minutes earlier George came in for the second time to make up the bar fire. Lobbin was back now and talking to Bullamy. Doris and Vivienne were busy serving a number of new arrivals. There was a loud buzz of conversation above which could be heard Mrs Bullamy's hearty laugh.

At nine-thirty Carolus said good-night to Doris and went out. He was pleased to find that a wind had risen and that it was a dark blustering night, not, probably, as windy as the night of the murder but with conditions similar enough to give point to his re-enactment of the movements of the murdered man.

He did not hurry down the road which led to the sea, remembering that Rafter had walked 'as though he was holding on to a rail'. It took him the best part of ten minutes to reach the promenade.

It was now that Rafter had met the policeman but tonight no figure in uniform was in sight. The promenade in fact seemed deserted.

After pausing for a few moments as Rafter had done, Carolus turned right and made his way against the wind towards the last shelter. But as he neared the first of the intervening shelters he saw a dark figure materialize from its shadows and found himself facing a solemn young policeman. It was clear that Sitwell had learned a lesson from his failure to discover the identity of the fat muffled man, and he scrutinized Carolus with suspicion before addressing him with somewhat exaggerated politeness.

" Good evening, sir," he said.

" Evening," said Carolus, who remembered John Moore's account of Sitwell. " Nice night for a murder, isn't it? "

Sitwell blinked.

" How d'you mean? " he said guardedly.

" Just my way of talking," said Carolus.

" We don't want any more murders," said Sitwell severely.

" No. You found the corpse, didn't you? "

Sitwell became an important public servant.

"I'm not saying whether I did or whether I didn't. We don't discuss such things."

"No? Pity. I'm interested."

"Oh, are you? Is that why you're hanging about here at the very time this murder was committed?"

"Yes," said Carolus. "That's why."

"I shall have to have your name and address," said Sitwell.

"Certainly. Did you ever see that little muffled-up man again, by the way?"

Sitwell stared.

"*What* little muffled-up man?" he asked haughtily.

"There surely wasn't more than one?"

"It seems to me," said Sitwell, "that you are altogether too inquisitive."

"You share the common opinion. Suppose I was to find the famous muffled-up man for you?"

Conflicting emotions were evidently tearing Sitwell to pieces. His official front must be maintained and yet if this person who seemed to know so much really could do what he suggested it would answer that still smarting reproof of Moore's.

"If you have any information," he said, "it's your duty . . ."

"I haven't, yet. But I have a feeling I may find this now almost legendary figure."

"In that case I hope you would report it immediately."

"To you?" asked Carolus mischievously.

"If I was the nearest police officer," said Sitwell. "Now may I have your name and address, sir? If you don't mind, that is."

Carolus gave them. He was interested to have learnt by inference that the muffled-up man had not yet been found.

"Would you tell me where you are going?" asked Sitwell.

"Certainly. To the farthest shelter. That is, if it's open to the public?"

Sitwell thought this levity in bad taste.

"Good night, sir," he said and continued on his way with slow dignified strides.

Carolus also went on, meeting no one else. As he passed each shelter he looked into it, as Sitwell must have done, but saw no one.

When he reached the farthest, the fateful shelter, he looked about him for a moment then sat in a corner out of the wind, the corner which, he judged, had been chosen by Rafter. Looking at his watch he saw that it was now 10.15.

It gave him a somewhat eerie feeling to realize that a few weeks ago a half-drunken man sitting where he was now had been battered to death. He thought how little he knew of the movements of the people involved at that time. Mrs Dalbinney and Emma Rafter were either leaving the promenade after their 'minute' there, or already on their way to Mrs Dalbinney's flat. The cinema they visited was nearly a mile from here at the other end of the promenade. They saw Lobbin during that minute, though half an hour later he was between this shelter and the bottom of Carter Street, since Sitwell met him thereabouts. Mr Morsell was relieving himself on the beach two shelters away while his wife waited near the public lavatory. Mr and Mrs Bullamy were on their way to the same point and noticing a stranger cross the road. If the Bullamys passed the Morsells neither couple noticed it, or admitted it afterwards. Mr Stringer was somewhere on the promenade, since Morsell met him there, but his exact movements were as yet unknown. Sitwell was in the town. Of the muffled-up man nothing was known except that Sitwell passed him nearly half an hour after this time and that he reached the shelter soon after Sitwell had found the body.

It was all very confusing and some of it almost inexplicable except by supposing that some lying had been done. Yet still Carolus could not imagine any of his new acquaintances in front of him with a coal-hammer, about to bring it down on a stupefied man's head.

He sat there for ten minutes and was about to move

when he saw someone approaching briskly. As he came nearer Carolus sat very still and tense, for it was a small fattish man who wore a scarf almost up to his eyes.

His pace never slackened till he reached the shelter. He seemed about to sit down, but becoming aware of Carolus he made a queer choking sound of surprise and stood staring.

" Good evening," said Carolus.

The man made no attempt to remove his muffler and his reply was a series of indistinct grunts which may have been meant for good evening.

" Nasty night," said Carolus.

" Flwbble," said the little man.

" Were you going to sit down? "

The sounds this time seemed to indicate a negative.

" This is where that murder was committed a few weeks ago," remarked Carolus.

" Flwbbffble," said the man, nodding doubtfully.

" Is this where Rafter was sitting? "

The scarf was not removed but Carolus gathered from the flwbble that the man did not know.

" But surely you must have seen where the corpse was when you found the policeman here? Before you went to telephone, I mean? "

The small man stared. Carolus could just see his eyes between the muffler and the rim of his hat and they were wide and startled.

" Flwbble, flwbble, flwbble," he said indignantly.

" You ought to meet Vivienne," said Carolus. " You two could have some delightful conversations."

The little man still stared. Then without another flwbble he turned and started back towards the town.

Carolus waited a full two minutes till the man was out of sight, then went into action. He ran swiftly back to where the road curved away from the promenade then crossed it and hurried on in the same direction, keeping to the pavement. He did not think the little man could have seen him so far, but he had to find that rotund small figure again without himself being seen. It might not, he thought, be easy.

12

F O R a time Carolus thought he had lost the little man, whose short legs moved at speed. Carolus did not return to the promenade itself but remained on the other side of the road which ran beside it, keeping in the obscurity of a shop entrance. He hoped to see him without himself being seen.

There was something very odd in the behaviour of this brisk and muffled person. On the night of the murder he had marched boldly up to the last shelter while Sitwell was there, and tonight he had returned to the promenade after Sitwell had completed his inspection. It could be quite innocent. He might be unaware that the police wanted to interview him. Or he might have some reason of his own for returning at a time when he hoped not to be seen. Again the fact that he had stopped short at the shelter when he had seen Carolus and appeared startled could be simply the reaction of a nervous man who remembered what had happened there, but it could be something else. If he was a creature of habit who always took his walk on the promenade at night, and had continued to do so since the murder, he must have taken great pains to dodge Sitwell. That again could be distaste for questioning or involvement, but there might be an uglier motive.

The whole thing was melodramatic and rather absurd, the scarf that was almost a mask, the muffled voice, the sudden departures of tonight and of the night of the crime, gave to this little noctambule something which intrigued Carolus but did not unduly raise his hopes. He could not think that the small man's information was going to solve his problem for him.

Besides it was beginning to be doubtful whether he

would see him again. It was useless to go out in search of him, for he might already have left the promenade and gone into the town and in any case Carolus wanted to follow him to his home without being seen.

It was nearly midnight before the man appeared as suddenly as before. His pace had not slackened. He materialized first near one of the shelters then marched boldly across the road. He did not look to right or left but kept his head down. He passed within ten yards of Carolus without apparently seeing him.

Carolus followed, keeping as far as he dared behind. But he had not far to go for when the small man had passed the Queen Victoria hotel he took a narrow turning to the right. Fortescue Street, noticed Carolus, and saw his quarry bolt like a rabbit into one of the small houses half way down. A light came on in an upper window which served as a beacon and approaching with a casual walk Carolus saw that it was number twenty-four.

Next morning he asked Mr Rugley about Fortescue Street.

"All due to be pulled down," he said. "They were mostly little apartment houses. It was where the theatricals used go before the old Theatre Royal became a cinema. They still let rooms in the summer but there's going to be a block of flats built there soon."

At number 24 Carolus found a card 'Apartments' in the window and rang the bell.

"Yes?" said a gaunt woman wearily as she looked round a half-open door.

"I want to see the gentleman on the first floor," said Carolus, remembering the lighted window of last night.

"Mr Biggett? He's not up yet. He doesn't get up till later."

"Perhaps you could tell him I want to see him urgently," suggested Carolus.

"Who shall I say?"

Carolus decided to take a chance. He felt instinctively that he would gain most by taking the offensive.

" Tell him the man he was talking to on the promenade last night," he said.

" You better come in then," said the landlady sulkily
and opened the door of the front room, which smelt of
flowerless plants and musty furniture. It was cold and
cheerless and keeping on his coat Carolus took a horse-
hair chair.

It was fully half an hour before the door opened and
a small men peered in. He was round-faced and round-
eyed and wore slippers and shabby clothes without a
collar and tie. He said nothing till Carolus began to
talk.

" Mr Biggett? I want a little talk with you. I'm investigating the murder of Ernest Rafter."

The voice when it came was scarcely more than a
whisper.

" Police? " said Mr Biggett.

Carolus pretended he had not heard this and and went
on forcefully.

" It's rather surprising that you have not come forward
to give information. You were the first on the scene except
for the policeman."

" Nobody asked me," said Biggett.

" But you must have known your information was
wanted. How long had you been on the promenade that
night? "

" About an hour. My usual time. It was not for me to
come forward. I've not moved from here."

" Had you been to that shelter earlier that evening? "

" Yes," said Biggett at once. " It was my turning point.
I walk first to that shelter, then right back to the jetty at
the other end of the promenade, then back to that shelter,
then home."

" Every night? "

" Yes."

" At the same time? "

" Very nearly. I like to stick to times and places."

" You have continued your walks since the murder? "

" Yes. A little later. The murder was nothing to do

with me. I did not want to be asked questions about it. I did not want to waste my time."

" Is your time so valuable, Mr Biggett? "

" To me, yes," said Biggett simply.

" May I ask what you do with it? "

" I have retired. I read and write."

" Write? " said Carolus, genuinely surprised.

" Yes. My journal. I have had a very interesting life. I was forty-two years with the same firm—of wholesale clothiers."

" How long have you lived here? "

" Oh, a very short time. A few weeks, in fact."

" You came from London? "

" Yes. I had a room in Hammersmith. My firm was at Shepherd's Bush."

Fascinated, Carolus questioned on.

" Had you been long in that room? "

" Twenty-eight years. It was handy for my place of employment."

" You are certainly a man of fixed habits, Mr Biggett. Forty-two years with one firm and twenty-eight in one room."

" It was more than that. I had my lunch in the same restaurant for eighteen years until it was pulled down and I went to another farther down the street. I bought my paper from the same shop for . . ."

" Yes, yes. It must have been quite a wrench for you to come here."

" I had been here for my summer holidays for thirty-five years," explained Mr Biggett, " so when I retired I naturally decided to live here."

" Of course. And you started your nightly stroll? "

" Oh no. I started that when I first came here on holiday after the First World War. At one time they extended the promenade, which changed things a little, but when I retired here my walk was taken all the year round instead of only during my summer holidays."

" I see. Did you see Ernest Rafter that night? "

Mr Biggett's soft voice never changed its mild tone.

" Not that night," he said. " I had seen him in the afternoon."

" What? "

" I travelled down with him on the 4.15. I had been to London to settle up some business and we travelled down together. Third class."

" How did you know it was Ernest Rafter? "

" He told me. We were alone in the compartment. He explained to me that he had been presumed dead and was now going to establish his right to his share of his father's money. He mentioned his two brothers and two sisters. They were, he said, somewhat parsimonious. He intended to get in touch with them at once."

Carolus, if not 'aghast', was greatly surprised at this gently spoken confidence.

" Where did you leave him? "

" At the station. I recommended him to the Queen Victoria Hotel."

" Did you see him pay for anything? "

" No. There was no occasion."

" You didn't see his pocket case or anything like that? "

" No," said Mr Biggett.

" Did you see him again? "

" Not alive. I saw only his huddled-up figure when he was dead, the policeman standing in the way. I did not know till the next day that it was the man with whom I travelled."

" Did you see anyone else on the promenade that evening? "

" I never see people when I'm walking, or not in the sense you mean. I walk, occasionally stopping to look at the sea."

" The policeman asked you to telephone the station? "

" He did. I complied, then came straight home."

" And that is all you know? "

" Certainly. I am not inquisitive. I am too occupied for that."

" Occupied? "

" My journal."

"This interview must be quite an interruption for you?"

"It has certainly disturbed my routine. I do not rise till 11.30. That is since retiring, of course. Previously I rose at seven-forty-five. I remain indoors till ten o'clock in the evening then take my walk. I go to bed at twelve-fifteen, read till one-fifteen, then sleep till eight o'clock."

"Suppose you are awakened?"

"I am not. For thirty-three . . ."

"Most interesting. Is there a coal-hammer in this house?"

"Certainly."

"You have seen it?"

"I have used it. In the coal-shed. It is still there. Did you suppose . . ."

"Mr Biggett, I have to ask that question of everyone connected with the case."

"But how am I connected with it?"

"You met Rafter that afternoon and received some confidences from him. You were on the promenade at the time of his murder."

"I do not see that either connects me. If a man cannot take a walk by the sea in the evening, what are we coming to?"

"Bedlam," said Carolus.

"Surely you would be well advised to search among those who had some motive for murdering Rafter, instead of coming to me."

"I don't know who may have had a motive."

"Then I suggest you find out. I have read every important murder case for the past forty years and I have never found one in which the murderer was not discovered through motive."

Carolus rose to go.

"I advise you to give your information to the police," he said stiffly, before leaving the house.

He phoned Mrs Dalbinney's flat at lunch time but there was no reply. It was not until the evening that his call was answered and then by the voice of a young man.

" Mrs Dalbinney? "

" Out," said the voice.

" Are you expecting her? This is Carolus Deene."

" Oh, Carolus. Do you remember me at Newminster? I'm Paul Dalbinney."

" I seem to recall a rather impudent boy in Hollingbourne's house."

" That sounds like me. What can I do for you? "

" I'd like to have what Mr Gorringer would call a Word with you."

" So would I. With you, I mean. Where are you staying? The Hydro? "

" No. The Queen Victoria."

" Ah yes. That's where this type stayed who is supposed to be my uncle. I see why you've chosen it. Shall I run round? "

" Later," said Carolus.

" What time? "

" Not before nine-thirty, if you don't mind."

" I'll be there."

Carolus went into the bar.

" You know what? " said Doris. " It's Christmas in three days' time and we haven't got a bit of holly up yet. I told Mr Rugley tonight and George is going to see to it tomorrow. How are you getting on with your old murder? Caught anyone yet? Vivienne says you never will, don't you, Vivienne? "

" Mmmm," assented Vivienne.

" She may well be right."

At nine-thirty almost to the moment Paul walked into the bar. He was a handsome youth with a lot of yellow hair and a healthy complexion.

" Hullo, Carolus," he said exuberantly. " This is something, isn't it? I never thought when you were boring me with history that you would be investigating the murder of my uncle. How does it go? "

" Slowly," said Carolus. " Where were you that night? "

" Oh round and about. I don't remember exactly."

" On the promenade at all? "

" I expect so. I saw this character, anyway. At least I suppose it was the one. I noticed these staring eyes they all talk about."

" Where was this? "

" I can't for the life of me remember. I just saw that face somewhere. But I don't see it can be much help to you. I didn't cosh him with a coal-hammer, you know. Though I might have if I'd known who it was. And if I'd had a coal-hammer, of course."

" You're very vague about your movements. Surely on the following day when you heard there had been a murder you must have recalled them carefully? "

" Not really. I'd had a couple of pints that night. But can you imagine the effect of the whole thing on the family? It kills me to hear them."

" Does it? "

" There's mother practically calling it a blot on the escutcheon. Aunt Emma feels it, quite sincerely, though. And in a different way so does Uncle Bertrand. It's startled the old boy out of his wits, I think. He lives very quietly with this young woman of his and doesn't want to be disturbed by his long-lost brother turning up and getting himself coshed."

" What about Locksley Rafter? "

" Oh he's a stick. Wait till you meet him. You never know what he's thinking. Stiff as a ramrod and never speaks if he can help it. I quite like the old boy but he used to scare me. You can imagine that this has been a blow to him, with a solicitor's practice in the district. It has to all of them, but I think Uncle Locksley is the most put out. Of course they're all as mean as sin. In their different ways. Mother's money-mean. Uncle Bertrand is generous in big things and mean in little ones . . ."

" You have all been questioned by the police? "

" Yes. That was a laugh, really. I honestly think they look on us as suspects."

" They do," said Carolus. " After all you are the only people known to have any reason to wish Ernest Rafter out of the way."

Paul laughed.

"But it's silly, Carolus. How were we to know some character who turned up in the town was Ernest? We didn't even know the sod was alive. And even if we had, *can* you imagine any of us banging him on the head? It's too far-fetched."

Carolus looked at his watch.

"Let's take a stroll," he said.

Paul followed him willingly enough.

"To the promenade?" he suggested.

"Why not?" agreed Carolus.

With any luck they would find Sitwell, he was thinking, and Sitwell might recognize Paul as the young man he had seen on the promenade on the night of the murder. Carolus resented the necessity for this when John Moore could tell him in a word whether or not Paul had been recognized, but his understanding with Moore was a firm one and he would not abuse it for the sake of a question so easily answered.

Sure enough Sitwell hove, as they say, into sight.

"Good-evening," said Carolus when they were level.

Sitwell's eyes were fixed on Paul.

"I've seen you before," he said wonderingly.

"Congratulations," said Paul cheekily. "Who is this character, Carolus?"

"You were down here on the night of the murder."

"Yes. Windy, wasn't it?"

"Have you been asked for a statement?"

"Of course. I made a beauty."

"But not," said Carolus coldly, "on the grounds that you were here on the promenade that night. You made it as one of the family."

"Was that it? These subtle distinctions between suspects are beyond me."

"They're not subtle. And in your case they are not distinctions. You are in both categories of suspect, that of people with a motive and that of being in the vicinity of the crime."

Paul whistled.

" I've practically got a noose round my neck, haven't I? "

" If you haven't told Detective Inspector Moore where you were that evening," said Sitwell ponderously, " I shall have to ask you to do so."

"That's all right," said Paul. " I rather like making statements. When do you suggest? "

" Mr Moore is in his office now."

" You mean . . ."

" Why not? " said Carolus. " Get it over."

" It's late," said Paul.

" Not very. It won't take long," Carolus reassured him.

" But what have I got to tell him? "

"That I don't know," said Carolus. " I expect he'll ask you among other things whom you met that evening."

" How on earth should I know? Really, what bores you all are with your eternal questions! I want to get to bed. However, I'll come quietly. I believe you let me in for this on purpose, Carolus."

" It's nothing to do with this gentleman," said Sitwell huffily. " It was I who recognized you. Please remember that."

Carolus watched while the two walked away side by side. He was about to follow when he saw a small round figure approaching at a brisk pace.

" Evening, Mr Biggett," he said.

Mr Biggett eyed him. In that uncertain light Carolus could not be sure but it seemed to him—perhaps it was his imagination—that there was a hint of triumph in the eyes visible between hat and scarf.

" Flwbble," replied Mr Biggett.

Nothing could be gathered from that.

13

CAROLUS realized rather wearily next morning that he must be conscientious and see the remaining two members of the family, Bertrand and Locksley Rafter, but he had a strong feeling that he was wasting his time in interviewing these people whose only known connection with the crime was something that was vaguely thought of as a motive, simply because no better motive had appeared.

That remained the crucial question—who in the world so much wanted this man's death that he was prepared to lure him to that lonely shelter and murder him in a brutal manner? It was, as Paul had said, frankly far-fetched to suppose that any member of this highly respectable family cared so much whether or not Ernest reappeared that he or she would carry out a scheme of this kind, even if he knew of the man's survival and arrival in Selby. But it was equally far-fetched, on the known facts, that anyone else would.

' I'll get it over ', he thought and made for Bertrand's house in Marine Square.

This was quite a sizeable Victorian house looking towards the sea, though some two hundred yards back from the promenade. All the houses in Marine Square were solid stucco erections with heavy metal balconies before their first-floor windows.

The interior was of a kind he knew well, the retired army officer's home, rich with the spoils of war and peace in the East. Magnificent rugs and elaborately beaten Indian silver, a profusion of teak and ivory, a scent of sandalwood and cigars, the atmosphere was rich and unmistakable.

But Bertrand Rafter when he appeared was not the typical retired officer. He was neat and clean-shaven, young-looking for fifty, with a pleasant friendly voice and manner. Carolus was at once at ease.

" Yes, I heard my sister had persuaded you to come over," said Bertrand. " I think it's very good of you. I hope the puzzle comes up to expectations? "

" It does."

" I feel we ought to be helpful but it's not easy. We lead pretty uneventful lives. Do you know all our movements at the time? "

" I don't know yours."

" If I've got the time right, I was in bed. I turned in at ten. My secretary, Molly French, lives here normally but she was in town that night so I was in the house alone from tea-time onwards. Fortunately I did not go out at all that evening. But I suppose that even the police could scarcely want alibis from us, so perhaps it doesn't matter that I have no witness to my early retirement."

" I don't know," said Carolus. " You see the wretched part of this case is that you and your family are the only people who have anything worth calling a motive."

" I know. It's absurd, but we can't get away from it. What makes it so fantastic is that obviously a murder would do more than anything to give publicity to Ernest's identity, as indeed it has done. ' Murdered man a Jap collaborator ', and so on. It was the very last thing any of us would have wanted. The money could have been arranged easily enough."

" Could it? "

" Oh yes. My father did not leave such a vast sum and my mother died after Ernest was presumed dead and never mentioned him in her will at all. I suppose that to get rid of Ernest we should all have been willing to contribute. We could have satisfied him, I think, and sent him back to Australia."

" You don't think he would have demanded more later? "

" No. He couldn't blackmail us. We should not have paid. After all, it would have been dangerous for him to reveal who he was and not by any means a matter of life and death for us. That is what we should have done if he had lived to approach us."

" I see your point though," said Carolus. " So far from having a motive for murdering Ernest you all had a very good motive for *not* murdering him, since his murder would do exactly what you did not want—call attention to him."

Bertrand smiled.

" I don't think we need take it so seriously," he said.

118

" It's so plain that we had nothing to do with it and did not even know he was alive. But I wish you could make the police see that."

" What do you think was the murderer's motive? " asked Carolus.

" Oh theft, probably. That seems to be the motive of most murders. Some thug who went out that night determined to rob the first person he saw."

" But the police do not think Ernest was robbed."

" Why not? "

" He had a pocket-case with seven pounds in it in his hip pocket and his wristwatch hadn't been taken."

" Seven pounds. A wristwatch. Modern thieves don't bother with such things. Ernest was probably robbed of a good sum."

" You think so? "

" Certainly. Find out what he had on him that night and you'll have your motive. Surely you or the police can do that."

" You may be right. Of course, the motive might have been revenge."

" You're thinking of this man Lobbin, who claims to have known him in Burma. Most unlikely I should have thought."

"Everything's most unlikely," said Carolus.

" I know Lobbin," said Bertrand. " A good fellow, I think. I hear he's in the bar of the Queen Victoria every night from opening to closing to escape from his wife, who nags him. Not at all the type for a murderer."

They were interrupted by the entrance of Molly French. She was an extremely attractive young woman with a frank cheerful face and good movements. Carolus was glad to see that Bertrand Rafter made no attempt to conceal their relationship, which seemed a very happy one.

" Deene is working on the murder," Bertrand explained, ' and we've been trying to find a motive. He has not yet asked where you were on the night of the crime."

" In London," she said. " Staying with my sister. It's a

pity, really, or I could have supplied Bertrand with an alibi. I've always wanted to be someone's alibi. It sounds so intimate."

" He doesn't think he needs one," said Carolus.

" But it's a good thing I didn't go down to the promenade that night as I sometimes do," said Bertrand. " Then I would have been suspect number one in this Alice-in-Wonderland affair."

They had a drink together and chatted rather aimlessly about the case for a while.

" I've only got three more interviews," Carolus said. " Then I think I've exhausted all I can do. If ever there was a case for the police, with all their resources, and for no one else, this is it. I'm sorry in a way that I started."

" Who are your interviews with? " asked Molly.

" Mr Locksley Rafter . . ."

" Oh *no*! " said Bertrand. " You can't suppose my poor brother had anything to do with it!

" He might have some information," said Carolus. " Perhaps without knowing it. At all events, in the interests of thoroughness I can't leave him out. Then there's a man called Stringer."

" I don't know him," Bertrand said.

" You wouldn't. He's an assistant in an ironmonger's shop."

" You are going to find out who bought the coal-hammer? "

" No. Not that. But this man was among those on the promenade that night."

" I see. Suspect by propinquity, not by consanguinity? " said Bertrand, rather pleased with his remark.

" I don't know what to consider a suspect at all," admitted Carolus. " The whole town's suspect, so far as I'm concerned."

" Why limit it to the town? " asked Bertrand. " There is transport, you know. Why not the whole country? "

" One must prod about somewhere. Thanks for what you've told me—and the drink. I'll let you know if I get any farther."

"You haven't told us who the third interview is with," said Molly French as they came to the front door.

"Oh, Lobbin, I suppose," said Carolus.

"Is he seriously suspected?"

"I don't know, but I should think so. He knew Ernest in Burma and probably suffered by his collaboration. He is thought to have recognized him that evening. And he was on the promenade at the relevant time. He is the only person known to fulfil all the three conditions."

"He has always seemed a very decent fellow to me," said Bertrand.

"Oh, by the way," said Carolus, "there is one routine question I must ask. Have you got a coal-hammer similar to the one used by the murderer?"

"We don't use coal," said Bertrand. "We're all-electric. And we're not very handy with tools in this house. I doubt if we've a hammer at all but we can look in what is euphemistically known as the tool-chest, if you like."

He led them to a small cold room at the back of the house and opened a drawer there which held the usual miscellany of household ironmongery. Among the blunt chisels and rusted screwdrivers was a fairly heavy hammer.

"We're better off than I thought," said Bertrand. "But the one used was surely heavier than this?"

"I haven't seen it but I should think so," said Carolus.

Before he left they had asked him to lunch with them on Christmas day, an invitation which Carolus readily accepted. The thought of roast turkey at the Queen Victoria hotel was not very attractive.

He went to his car and drove off in the direction of Bawdon. He had decided to make his visit to Locksley Rafter unannounced and take the chance of not being able to see him.

Bawdon, he found, was just nine miles away. It was the county town and Carolus passed the Sessions House on his way to the offices of Rafter and Mohawk. These were on the ground floor of a large Georgian house.

Rather to his surprise he was shown in to Locksley

Rafter's room at once. It was large and comfortable, refreshingly free from files and documents.

No family likeness was noticeable in Locksley, though in the few words he spoke Carolus could hear the rich and plummy accent he had noted in the voices of Emma, Bertrand and Isobel Dalbinney. He wondered whether Ernest had spoken like this, too.

"You know why I've come to see you, Mr Rafter?"

The spare, thin-lipped solicitor said, "I do."

"I may say at once that I am having a very difficult time with this case, which your sister asked me to investigate. May I ask you a number of questions?"

"You may."

"They will probably seem absurd to you as they have seemed to your brother and sisters. But if I am to get anywhere at all I must know what were the movements of each member of the family on the day of the murder. I understand you called on Mrs Dalbinney that day?"

"I did."

"Do you remember when you reached Selby?"

"At four."

"And your sister's flat?"

"At four-five."

"You remained until?"

"Approximately six."

"You had your car?"

"I had."

"And after you left your sister you drove straight home?"

"I did not."

"Perhaps you called on some other members of your family?"

"No.'

"Where did you go, Mr Rafter?"

"To the Hydro."

"You dined there?"

"I did."

"And then?"

"A film."

"At the Palatine?"

"No. The Regalia."

"At what time did you come out?"

"At ten-fifteen."

"Then what?"

"Home."

"So you were in before eleven?"

"No, a puncture."

"You stopped to change a wheel?"

"I did."

"And reached home?"

"Eleven-thirty."

"Was Mrs Rafter at home at the time?"

"In bed."

"You woke her?"

"I did not."

"Can you provide any sort of evidence of all this?"

"None."

"This is most unfortunate. It means that, however far-fetched it may seem to you, it was possible, so far as can be shown, for you to have committed the murder. I was hoping you would have a clear alibi."

"Unnecessary," said Locksley Rafter without the least emotion.

"It may seem so to you. But you and your family are almost the only people who are considered to have any motive for killing this man."

Locksley astonished Carolus by asking a question.

"What motive?"

"I don't think I need go into that. His return could not have been welcome to you. Did you know he was still alive?"

"I did not."

"Did you go on the promenade at Selby that night?"

"No."

"Or anywhere near it?"

"Yes."

"Where was that?"

"The car park."

"Which car park was it?"

"Near the Hydro."

"That is the one by the little garden which divides the road from the promenade? A minute's walk, in fact, from the shelter in which your brother was found murdered?"

"Exactly."

"Did you see anyone about when you went to get your car?"

"No."

"That would have been when you left the Regalia Cinema at a quarter past ten?"

"Approximately."

"You realize that somewhere round this time your brother was being murdered?"

"I do."

"You heard and saw nothing that could be connected with this?"

"Nothing."

"I see you have electric heating here. Do you use coal at home?"

"We do not."

"You have never had a hammer such as the one used?"

"Never."

"Mr Rafter," said Carolus desperately. "You have answered every question I have put to you and your answers may have been quite accurate. But have you nothing to tell me which may be of assistance?"

"Nothing."

"Have you any opinion about this murder?"

"None."

"What did you think of your brother Ernest?"

"A louse."

"Have you always thought that? Or was it his reported behaviour as a prisoner of war which makes you say it?"

"From childhood."

"You felt no sorrow at all at his death?"

"Sorrow? None."

"But it was an inconvenience. The publicity and so on. Is that it?"

"Precisely."

"Do you suspect anyone?"

"Yes."

"Who?"

"Lobbin."

"Really?" said Carolus, delighted to come on anything as human as suspicion. "On what grounds?"

"Motive. Ability. Opportunity."

"I see what you mean. But doesn't it, all the same, seem rather improbable to you?"

"No."

Carolus rose to go.

"Thank you for all your co-operation," he said ironically.

"Delighted," replied Locksley Rafter and with a curt nod to Carolus picked up and began to study some papers.

There remained Stringer and on his way back to Selby Carolus decided that he would see him today, so that with the exception of Lobbin his interrogatees would all be disposed of.

He found Stringer's home—a council house on the outskirts of the town. The door was opened by three jam-stained children who fixed him with the cold insolent stare of creatures hypnotized by curiosity.

"Is your father in?" asked Carolus.

Their eyes did not leave him. There was no motion among them. They seemed not even to blink. One raised his voice.

"Dad!" he said and continued to watch Carolus.

"What is it?" came a male voice from within.

"A man," said the child.

"Coming," said the voice, and all became still.

Mr Stringer when he presented himself was in shirt-sleeves. He looked what Mr Morsell had called him 'a good quiet little man, fond of reading'.

"Yes?" he said peering myopically at Carolus over the heads of his children.

"Could I have a few words with you alone?"

"Are you the gentleman the Reverend Morsell told me about?"

"I shouldn't be surprised."

"Enquiring into something we won't mention before the children?"

"Well . . ."

"If so, I'm sorry but there's nothing I can tell you."

"But there is. I understand you were on the promenade that night."

"Ush," said Mr Stringer sibilantly. "I don't want them to know anything about it."

"Then send them away," said Carolus growing, for once, a little irritated.

"It wouldn't do any good. I'm not to discuss it."

"Who said not?"

"Mr Morsell for one. And there's nothing to tell you for another."

"But you were down there, weren't you?"

"Down where? I've nothing to say and that's my last word."

"I shall have to inform the detective inspector investigating the case that you decline to give information."

"You inform him," challenged Mr Stringer. "I've nothing to hide."

"Then why not answer a couple of questions?"

"Because not," said Mr Stringer.

One of the motionless children uttered again.

"What's he want, dad?"

"Never you mind," said Mr Stringer.

"Perhaps I could call on you at the shop?" tried Carolus.

"You would be wasting your time. I've told you I've got nothing to say."

"I could at least buy a coal-hammer there."

"No you couldn't, because we've none in stock. I sold the last one to . . ."

"Yes, Mr Stringer?"

"To the Reverend Morsell, if you want to know."

"Thank you," said Carolus, "and good evening to you."

14

IF his last two interviews had been difficult, they were nothing to the one that awaited him that evening. He was warned as soon as he entered the bar by Doris, now a firm ally if not a fellow conspirator.

"You better watch your p's and q's," she told him. "She's on the warpath after you. She's been in once this evening threatening I don't know what and I shouldn't be surprised if she comes in again. I told her, we don't want any trouble in here, I said, but you know what she is."

"I don't even know *who* she is," said Carolus.

"Oh, go along. That Bella Lobbin, of course. She says you've been saying things about her husband. I suppose she thinks *she's* the only one that can go for him."

Carolus sat down in a corner but he had not long to wait. The door from the street was thrown open and a red-faced stringy woman with prominent teeth and furious eyes pushed her way in.

"Is that him over there?" she asked the room at large and without waiting for an answer crossed and stood over Carolus. "What have you been saying about my husband?" she asked loudly.

"If you like to tell me his name I may be able to help you."

"Never mind his name!" shouted Mrs Lobbin. "And I don't want any help from you, thank you. What have you been saying about him?"

"Now Mrs Lobbin!" called Doris.

"Oh, Lobbin," said Carolus, as though it had just dawned on him. "Poor fellow," he added feelingly.

" I'll give you poor fellow if you're not careful! " went on Mrs Lobbin with more verbosity than coherence. " Going round taking anyone's character away! There ought to be law against it."

" There is," said Carolus.

" It's a pity you don't follow it then. I've never heard anything like it. My husband's a good man and wouldn't hurt anyone let alone bang them on the head with a hammer, and here you go saying the police are after him and I don't know what not. What's it to do with you, anyway? "

" Nothing, really."

" Then why don't you keep your nose out of it? That's what I want to know. Anybody would think you'd got a right to say things that aren't true. If there's any more of it you'll have me to answer to."

" Have a drink? " suggested Carolus.

" I wouldn't touch your drink, not if you was to pay me."

" Just a small one? "

" I'll have a rum," said Bella angrily. " I call it real low-down of you to pick on him," she continued, as though to show that her acceptance of a drink in no way weakened her case. " He hasn't done anything to you, has he? "

" Nothing at all."

" You ought to be ashamed of yourself, talking like that about anyone," went on Bella Lobbin, her fury unabated as she received her glass of rum with a quick nod. " You'd very soon get into trouble if I had my way. Cheerio. Here's the best. You know very well my husband never had anything to do with it yet you go on blacking his name as though he was a crimingle."

" But Mrs Lobbin . . ."

" Don't Mrs Lobbin me. I've heard what I've heard and I'm not going to stand for it. I'll tell you that. He's got quite enough ideas in his head as it is."

Carolus, accustomed to pick up irrelevancies of this sort, said, " What kind of ideas? "

"Writing and that. He thinks he ought to have been a writer, if you please. Still, that doesn't make him a murderer."

"No. Not necessarily," agreed Carolus. "What sort of things did he write?"

"Don't ask me!" said Bella Lobbin. "It's bad enough to be married to anyone like that. Scribble, scribble, scribble. I don't know. But it's no reason for you to run round saying he did for this Ernest Rafter."

"But Mrs Lobbin, I said nothing of the sort."

"Next best thing you did. The police were after him for it, you said."

"He is certainly one of the suspects."

"There you go again! 'Suspects'! Who's a suspect, that's what I want to know. If my husband's a suspect, how is it we've got our coal-hammer all this time? Answer me that. I keep it in the shop now to show people. With all this talk going round you have to do something. There you are, I say. What's that, if my husband did it? It's never been out of the house, I say, so I'd like to know how it can have been used for the murder. Besides, the police have got the one it was done with. I saw it at the inquest."

"But your husband was seen on the promenade that night, Mrs Lobbin."

"Well, I've told him often enough not to go wandering about at night. But that's what he's like. I want to think, he says. Think! It's a pity he doesn't think of his business a bit more. Anyway, it's no excuse for you saying all sorts of things about him." Carolus saw the resentment being brought back with artificial respiration. It was evident that Bella Lobbin had not said all she had promised herself to say. "What right *have* you to go telling people he's a suspect? It only needs a little talk like that to have the police round again asking questions. You ought to know better. Yes, I will have another. Besides, there's more than meets the eye in all this. What about that Mrs Dalbinney? After the way she behaved to me I'd believe anything of her."

"Didn't you rather invite it, Mrs Lobbin?"

"What do you mean invite it? I told her what I thought of her, if that's what you mean, same as I'm telling you. I'm not one to keep anything to myself when I know I'm in the right. You know very well you've got no business to come interfering. Cheerio. All the best. The sooner you go back to where you come from the better for everyone, if you ask me."

There was a long smouldering pause.

"And anyway, why couldn't you ask my husband to his face if you had anything to say, instead of going behind his back talking about him?"

"I will," promised Carolus.

Mrs Lobbin finished her rum and rose to go. But for the benefit of those who had heard her outburst she could not leave without showing that she was no whit mollified by two rums, and meant to have the last word.

"So you mind what you're saying," was her good-bye to Carolus, as with flushed face she stood over him. "Else I won't be answerable."

On that she marched out.

"What did I tell you?" asked Doris. "Can you wonder at him spending his evenings in here when he's got her at home nagging at him all the time? It's a wonder he hasn't done something before now. He'll be in presently, poor fellow, glad to get away for a bit. She very seldom comes in here, I will say that. They live over the shop and I think she has a bottle there when she wants it."

When Lobbin entered he looked round to find Carolus then came straight to him.

"I'm afraid my wife has been trying to pick a quarrel with you," he said. "I'm sorry if she said anything out of place. She gets ideas in her head."

"That's what she told me about you," said Carolus smiling.

"Oh, that. No, I mean she gets hold of something and can't let it rest. I've tried to make her see that you and the police are bound to want to know all about those who were on the prom that night, but she won't see it.

Now I'm perfectly willing to tell you anything you want to know."

"Thanks. I'd like very much to hear what you knew of Ernest Rafter."

"I was a p.o.w. with him. That's all."

"He behaved badly?"

"That's an old story and he's dead now. I don't want to rake up details. But there's no doubt about it he was in with the Japs."

"And you suffered from it?"

"Look, Mr Deene, those of us who went through all that want to forget it. Most of us have forgotten it—except sometimes, at night. There's no point in trying to fix the blame. Rafter collaborated and that's that."

"You bore no grudge?"

"I'd long since forgotten all about it."

"Until?"

"Until one day the name suddenly connected in my mind with this family here."

"And you told Mrs Dalbinney. Why did you choose her?"

"She's a lady," said Lobbin simply. "Anyway, I didn't know the others much then. Bertrand's only taken to coming to the shop lately and Miss Rafter I just knew by sight."

"Mrs Dalbinney asked you to say nothing about it?"

"Yes. She did. And I wouldn't have if my wife hadn't got hold of the story and gone round there and made a fuss. I told you she gets ideas in her head. Before I knew where we were it was all over the town."

"But you had no idea that Ernest Rafter was still alive?"

"Not before that night, I hadn't."

"That *night*. You recognized him, then?"

"I wasn't sure at first. Well, I wasn't *quite* sure all along. I saw this man in here with those peculiar eyes he had and at first I just thought he was like Rafter. Then there was something about him I thought I knew. He seemed a lot older than when I knew him in Burma.

When I knew him he looked quite a young man. Now he looked old and kind of bitter. It took me some time to be sure it was the same."

"But you were sure in the end?"

"Yes, because I asked Doris his name."

"So what did you do?"

"Do? Nothing. I had my own troubles that night."

"You didn't think to let the Rafters know their brother was here?'

A smile crossed Lobbin's rugged and untidy face.

"The last time I did that it led to trouble so I wasn't going to have that again. I kept what I thought to myself. But I did wonder what the family would do when they knew he was here."

"He didn't recognize you?"

"I shouldn't think so. He didn't say anything, anyway. He was knocking them back pretty fast."

"You saw him leave the bar?"

"I didn't notice him going. But at some time before ten I saw he wasn't there any more. I asked Doris when he'd left and she said—'oh a long time ago'."

"You waited till closing time?"

"Pretty well. I usually do. Then I went for a walk."

"Which way did you take?"

"Not towards this shelter where the man was found. Right up the other way towards the Palatine cinema."

"See anyone you knew?"

"Yes. Mrs Dalbinney and her sister. It looked as though they'd just come out of the cinema. When I saw them they were walking back across the road from the prom."

"But, Mr Lobbin, why didn't you tell them then that their brother was still alive?"

"Me? After what happened before? Not likely. I just kept going as fast as I could. I didn't want any more of that. They'd hear soon enough, I thought."

"They certainly did. But it must have been almost irresistible to tell them then."

"No, Mr Deene. I'd seen what had come of my putting

my nose in before. I just said good-evening and set off walking in the opposite direction."

"Towards the shelter where the body was found?"

"Well, that way."

"Who did you meet this time?"

"I met Mr and Mrs Bullamy."

"Again, you didn't say anything to them?"

"No. They were over on the other side near the sea."

"They say they didn't see you."

"Quite likely they didn't."

"How far did you go towards the shelter?"

"Not very far. Three or four shelters away. Then I turned back and met a young policeman. Then I went home."

"I don't quite see why you went down there at all, Mr Lobbin."

"I didn't want to go home straight away. Everything was shut."

"There's another thing I'd like to ask you about. It's a bit personal but you've invited me to ask you any questions I like. During the evening did you leave here for a while and return?"

"I did, yes."

"What was that for?"

"Well, Mr Deene, I can't deny my wife and I have a bit of a row every once in a while. We had one that evening. When I came out I left her—well, storming, if you know what I mean. I thought I'd just run round and see if she'd got over it. It's only a few doors away."

"And had she?"

"No. Worse than ever. You've seen what she's like. So I left her to it and came back here. When closing time was coming round I thought I wouldn't go back there till she was asleep."

Carolus gave him a friendly smile.

"You account for your movements very well," he said, "but so does everyone else in this damned case."

They had a drink together, then, as if touching on a far less solemn subject, Carolus said—"I hear you write."

"Not really. Little bits when they come to me. I'd like to have been a writer, though. I think I might have been if I hadn't got married. I seem to be able to imagine things."

"Fiction?"

"I suppose you'd call it that. I just make things up out of my head and put them on paper."

"Do you keep them afterwards?"

"Some of them I do. Other things I destroy as soon as I've finished them."

"You've never tried to publish?"

"Well, the *Selby-on-Sea Advertiser* put in a little bit I wrote about the smugglers that were supposed to be here in the old days. Nothing else."

"You've written nothing about the murder?"

"Oh no. These are things I imagine. I wouldn't want to write about anything like that."

"I gather your wife doesn't approve much of your writing?"

"It's not really in her line. She's got other things to think about."

"Haven't we all?" said Carolus feelingly.

Indeed he decided, as he slowly undressed and got into bed that night, he had almost too much to think about.

A number of people *could* have killed Ernest Rafter but they were all unlikely and there did not seem, when he considered the matter dispassionately, any real motive attributable to any of them. It simply was not credible that one of the family, put out by the return of this inconvenient relative, should have gone out with a hammer and committed this particularly violent crime in order to save themselves money, even if they were aware of his survival. It simply was not credible that Lobbin, whom Carolus judged a mild and long-suffering man, should have been so overcome with rage and hatred at the sight of a man who had been 'in with the Japs' nearly twenty years ago that he had gone home to fetch his weapon, then guessing that Ernest had gone down to the promenade, marched up and down until he had found and slain him.

It simply was not credible that Bodger, mysteriously informed about the presence of a collaborator in Selby, had gone out that night and killed him to avenge his son, however dearly he had loved the young man.

As for those with no known motive, they were even more unlikely. It was, Carolus supposed, just conceivable that Moore's investigation into Ernest's past would show that he had known the Bullamys in Australia, though as they had pointed out it was a continent with nine million inhabitants, and even if they were acquainted and did recognize Ernest in the bar that night, were they the sort of people to make a joint effort to kill him? Besides, how could they have become suddenly provided with the weapon when they were staying a long way from the Queen Victoria?

So far as Carolus knew, neither the Morsells nor Stringer had any motive at all, but even if one of them had, was it possible to think of them as potential murderers? The thing became more and more fantastic when one thought of it in these terms and even if Mr Biggett had formed a violent prejudice against Ernest during their train journey, or had discovered something about him which he thought quite dreadful, one could not see the little man wielding a hammer.

That was what made the case so infuriating, no one seemed to have a motive worth the smallest risk. If it was in fact robbery, as Bertrand had suggested, it must be someone who knew about that envelope full of treasury notes. But it had not the *feel* of a murder for the sake of robbery.

Why then, had Ernest been killed? That was the crucial question and suddenly as he thought about it Carolus caught a glimmering of a possible answer.

Suppose, his tired mind suggested, suppose there was *no* reason? Suppose this was simply murder for the sake of murder? All his life as an investigator Carolus had wondered what would happen if such a thing came about. Could this at last be the case of which the very idea had so long intrigued him?

If it was, it had the effect of eliminating the suspects who were there for the sake of their possible motive. What was worse, it opened the field beyond all reason. *Anyone* could have killed Ernest Rafter that night, for there was no reason to think that the murderer had been seen. He could have been waiting on the beach or in the gardens until someone came to the shelter.

Surely, thought Carolus, this way madness lies. Who would plan and carry out an indiscriminate murder just for the sake of it? It *had* been done, but by paranoiac undergraduates in America where crime was known to take the weirdest forms.

He tried to keep his head. Could he be finding his way towards the truth at last? Once before, when he first saw the shelter, the ghost of a premonition had come to him, but he had put it aside as monstrous and far-fetched. Now it seemed, as compared with the fearful *non sequiturs* of normal deduction in this case, at least a tenable theory.

Before sleeping he decided to return to it in the cold light of day and perhaps try it out on Bertrand, who struck him as having a cool and steady brain. Then he would know better if it was more than fantasy.

Of one thing Carolus felt certain before he slept. If this was the truth, the murderer was almost certain to escape. No detective force on earth could discover him. For the perfect murder was the murder without motive.

15

ON Christmas morning Carolus went into the bar with a present each for Doris and Vivienne. He had half an hour to pass before going to lunch at Bertrand Rafter's.

Doris was ecstatic.

" Oh, isn't that lovely! " she said. " I *do* think it's kind of you. I've always wanted one like that. I'm sure I never dreamt of any such thing. I don't know how to thank you. I shall show my mother that when I get home. Fancy you thinking of it! It's very extravagant of you, too, and I oughtn't really to have let you do it. I never guessed for a moment you were going to do anything like that. Thank you ever so much."

Carolus was waiting for a grateful mmmm from Vivienne, but he had a surprise.

"Thank you very much, Mr Deene," she said quite clearly. "It's very kind of you and I like it ever so much."

"Let me see," said Doris. "Oh, isn't it pretty! It will go lovely with your eau-de-nil, won't it, Vivienne?"

"Mmmm," said Vivienne, but with animation.

"Now you've got to have one with me," said Doris to Carolus. "Yes you have. A nice large Scotch, how you like it, with lots of soda. Here's a very happy Christmas to you, I'm sure. You're not bothering your head about that old murder today, are you?"

"No," said Carolus smiling.

He drove to Marine Square. The door of Bertrand's house was opened by Molly, who looked fresh and handsome. She led him to the large ground-floor sitting-room, where there was a sensible display of bottles. Bertrand was jovial and welcoming and they sat down to wait for lunch.

"Molly's bribed our crone to come in for the morning," said Bertrand, when Molly French had left the room, "so we're having lunch sharp at one, to let her wash up and get home to do her own family's dinner. Do you understand these mysteries?"

"I'm very lucky," Carolus said; "I've a married couple who have been with me for years."

"Oh yes. My sister told me. They don't approve of you investigating murders, I gather. And talking of murders are you making any progress with ours?"

"No practical progress," said Carolus. "But last night I had a new and very extraordinary idea."

"Am I going to hear it?"

"In confidence, yes. It's too fanciful and too macabre to be anything but an idea at the moment, but I'd like to try it out, as it were, by telling you about it. It is, briefly, this. We've spent a lot of time in this case trying to discover who had a motive for murdering Ernest Rafter, or trying to see how someone with a motive could have been anywhere near the last shelter at the time. It has led us into such absurdities as to think of your sisters as possible suspects or to suppose that someone like Bodger or Lobbin might have done it out of hatred for a collaborator. But suppose, for a moment, we forget the motive or go a step further and imagine that there *was* no motive. What then?"

"The act of a maniac, you mean?"

"Some kind of maniac, I suppose, yes. Suppose someone with no motive at all for killing your brother was waiting down in that shelter for the first victim who came along . . ."

"Oh come now, Deene. This is fantastic."

"Yes," said Carolus sadly, "I suppose it is. Now I come to express it in words it is far-fetched. But so is every other theory in this damned case. I rather liked this one when I thought of it last night."

Bertrand smiled.

"I rather like it, too," he said. "The trouble is that nothing could make me believe it. It's a pretty idea and it would put a stop to all this nonsense about my family and Lobbin and Bodger, but it has a fictional taste about it, hasn't it?"

"I suppose you're right."

"Anyway, if it were true, how would you go about finding your man? It might be absolutely anyone."

"Yes. That's the thing. Unless by any chance he was seen."

"Seen? But wouldn't you know by now?"

"There were several people about on the promenade that night," said Carolus. "And one was seen crossing the road, by some strangers to the place. It's possible that if we could get any sort of lead on him they would be able to identify him and for the police the rest would be easy. They've probably got technical stuff from the shelter with their microscopes and whatnot. But that is supposing a great deal. My notion may be nonsense and even if it isn't, how are we ever going to know who to put up for these people to identify? "

" I see that."

" Even if we pre-suppose this monster who kills for pleasure, we don't know whether it's a man or woman. Those blows on the head of a half-drunk man could have been dealt by a woman as well as a man."

" What about the man crossing the road? "

" I suppose that could have been a woman, too, dressed as a man. But there is no absolute reason to suppose that was the murderer. The murderer could have got away by the beach or the garden."

" It's damned interesting," said Bertrand. " I can only wish you luck with it. How did you get on with my brother Locksley? "

" A bit monosyllabic, isn't he? But he answered every question I put to him. He seemed almost anxious to show that so far as circumstances went he could have committed the crime."

Bertrand laughed.

" That's rather like him," he said. " He looks for a challenge. I wonder what *he* would think of this new theory of yours."

" I imagine he'd say ' tenable ' or ' untenable ' and that is all we should know."

Molly came to call them to lunch and over the turkey and champagne the talk grew reminiscential.

" Locksley is the eldest of us," said Bertrand. " He seemed almost grown-up to me, though there are only five years between us. Isobel came between us; she's a year older than I. Then after two or three years came Emma and Ernest with one year between them.

" I'm afraid Ernest was always the outcast. As the youngest boy he should have had the most fuss made of him but as a small child he was horribly petulant and selfish and never really changed. He was such a sneak too. Locksley and I would do some devilry and Ernest would tell my father at once.

"But Emma stood up for him. They had nothing in common that I could see, for Emma loved animals and Ernest showed no interest in them, Emma was straight as a die and Ernest inclined to be dishonest, yet she always tried to protect him from our ragging. Even when we began to hear those fearful stories about Ernest during the war Emma refused to believe them for a long time. I daresay she would like to think the best of him now."

"So your sister Emma is the one with whom Ernest would have got in touch, if he got in touch with anyone?"

"Yes. And she is the one who would have given him money."

"Is it possible, do you think, that Ernest was in touch with your sister? That she never told you about this, and afterwards was afraid to admit it because she thought it might involve her whole family?"

Bertrand looked up shrewdly.

"You put me in a difficult position," he said. "I can only say you must ask her."

"Yes of course. Thank you. I will."

"But all that won't do much to advance your new theory."

"Nothing will do much to advance that, I fear. The detective inspector in charge of the case is a friend of mine but he is apt to think I'm too imaginative. If I were to go to him and say I thought that the murder was committed without a motive and ask him to hold an all-embracing identity parade so that the couple who saw someone crossing the road that night could pick out their man or woman he would laugh, I'm afraid."

"I suppose he might. But it's worth a chance, surely. Even if you had to drag in half the population of Selby."

They chattered on rather aimlessly until Carolus was about to leave them.

"I wonder if you'd mind dropping me at my parents' place," said Molly. "I must go and see them. I always have to spend Christmas evening with them, which is a bore for Bertrand. It's not very far from you, in Prince Albert Mansions."

Carolus said he would be delighted and Molly climbed in beside him.

"I wish you could get this thing cleared up," she said. "It's wretched for them all. Isobel particularly. And I think Locksley feels it more than he shows."

"I should have thought the harm was done," said Carolus. "I don't see that finding the murderer is going to make it much easier for them."

"I do. It's the doubt. They don't know the police are not going to do something silly."

"John Moore, who is in charge of the case, is a very sound man. The last person to try to fake up evidence or charge anyone till he is sure where he stands."

"All the same," said Molly charmingly, "it's you we're counting on."

"I'll do my best," promised Carolus.

That evening he was delighted to see Emma Rafter coming into the bar leading her Boxer. He did not hesitate or prevaricate but opened the matter straight away.

"Miss Rafter," he said. "I think you knew of your brother Ernest's presence in England before the night he was murdered."

She paled a little but said nothing.

"Looking back on our conversation," went on Carolus, "I realize that you never said in so many words that this was not so. But I would ask you to tell me the whole truth of the matter now."

She looked Carolus straight in the face.

"I will," she said. "I have never been *out* of touch with Ernest. I have had to write to him under many names and in several countries, but ever since he first went to Australia after the war he has kept in touch with me."

"Have you kept his letters?"

"Unfortunately, no. I was afraid someone would find them. You see no one else knew he was alive. I never mentioned it to my brothers or to my sister or to anyone else in the world. It was far best for them to think him dead. The only difficulty was the money my father left. When he was to be 'presumed dead' I wondered what I ought to do. I thought he could never admit his identity and turn up, but I did not want to benefit from his share. So I sent him at once the amount by which the distribution of his share among us had increased my own. Since my father's will benefited us all equally, his fifth had been divided between the remaining four. So I could see by how much mine was increased and sent it to him. Then when my mother died and left a much larger sum of money, I was able to make up to Ernest *all* that he had lost by being presumed dead when my father died. None of the others knew anything about this. None of them dreamt for a moment he was still alive."

" Until? "

" Until after he had been found murdered."

" But you knew he was in England? "

Emma Rafter hesitated then very quietly said, " Yes. I knew."

" He wrote to you from his hotel in King's Cross? "

" Yes."

" And you sent him some more money? "

" Yes. He promised to go away. I did not want my brothers and sister to know. He promised faithfully that he would leave at once. But as you know, he did not keep his promise. His word was never worth much, but that time I did believe he'd keep it."

" It cost him his life, that broken promise."

" Yes."

" He did not tell you he was coming down to Selby? "

" No. I thought he had left for Australia. I heard nothing at all."

" So what you told me was true, Miss Rafter? You were in this bar with him without knowing it? "

" Of course it was true. I don't lie. I was here only for a few minutes and noticed nobody. I wanted a quick drink before my evening with Isobel."

" And when you heard about the murder? What then? "

" I was sorry. I knew that once again Ernest had broken his word. I guessed he had come down here to put pressure on the family. I saw it all. Yet I was sorry. It was a dreadful way to die."

"Yes. Did you eventually tell your family you had been in touch with Ernest?"

Emma smiled rather sadly.

"I think they guessed it," she said. "Or rather Bertrand did. He knew I was fond of Ernest. It was just like an awful repetition of some situation in our childhood when I had managed to help him secretly. Or Bertrand may have heard about it at the bank—we're both friendly with Mr Bargiter the manager. Ernest asked for the money in cash so I drew it out and sent it to him by ordinary post. Bertrand told me I was a fool to send Ernest money, just as he used to tell me I was a fool to help him as a child."

"Bertrand knew you'd sent money, then?"

"Only afterwards. They none of them knew anything at all till after poor Ernest's death."

"Did you tell them then?"

"Bertrand seemed to know. He has always been able to see through me. He wasn't cross about it, though. Just told me I was silly to do it."

"Why didn't you admit it to me or to the police?"

"It seemed to involve us all more. Although I never dreamt that Ernest was in Selby that night, if they knew I was aware of his presence in the country they might have thought I'd told my family. Then the family *would* have been involved."

"And you really didn't tell the family or anyone, Miss Rafter? Honour bright?"

"Honour bright."

"I believe you," said Carolus.

"Do you imply that thousands wouldn't?"

"No. On the contrary I think the detective inspector investigating the case would."

"Would he? Bertrand wanted me to tell him frankly. Bertrand thinks nothing, anyhow, can involve the family and that I ought not to keep it from the police that I sent Ernest money."

"I think he's right. If I may so, Miss Rafter, it doesn't take a very shrewd person to know that you're speaking the truth. I don't think it will help the police much to know about that money, but it won't do you or your family any harm for them to know."

"Then I'd better tell them. Now I must run. I'm spending this evening at Isobel's."

"Please give her my Christmas wishes," said Carolus. "And young Paul."

"I will. You lunched with Bertrand today. How do you get on with Molly?"

"I think she's delightful.'

"So do I," confided Emma, "but of course Isobel disapproves. She won't divorce her own husband either."

"Catholic?" asked Carolus.

"High Church. So she has rather got it in for poor Molly, though they're very polite when they meet. Isobel, Paul, Peter and I went out to Locksley's today for our Christmas din. Tonight Isobel and I hope for a quiet evening. We look at television and play bezique. At the same time."

"Excellent," said Carolus.

When Emma had gone, Carolus went across to the counter.

"There you are!" said Doris in her warm, welcoming way. "I was wondering when you'd come across." She leaned over the counter, inviting Carolus to do the same. "There've been such ructions round at Lobbin's," she whispered. "Poor fellow, on Christmas day, too. He didn't tell me what it was about, but you should have seen his face when he came in. It is a shame, really, and such a nice quiet fellow. She can't leave him alone for five minutes. But today it must have been something out of the common because when he came in he looked like doomsday. He's only been here about half an hour. So now I suppose he'll mope in here all the evening till it's turning-out time. Look who's just come in!" It was Bodger. "I suppose on Christmas night I can't refuse to serve him, but he's got a cheek coming in after the last time. Yes, Mr Bodger?"

Bodger had a pint.

"There you are," said Doris, "but don't let me hear you say anything out of place, that's all." She returned to Carolus but not in whispered confidence. "We shall get a lot in tonight," she said "Always do, Christmas evening. That's Mr Stringer, just come in."

"Yes, I know him."

"He's very quiet, really. Likes a joke now and again, but never anything out of turn. Guinness, Mr Stringer? That's right."

"Reverend Morsell's coming in," said Stringer. "Just to show."

To show what, Carolus wondered. The flag? Willing? A leg? But he said nothing.

The Bullamys greeted him and wished him a happy Christmas. George came in to do the fire. Then, as if to complete the tally, Sitwell walked in wearing plain clothes and having a young woman with him. He gave Carolus a long stare in which there was no friendliness at all and sat down with his girl at a table.

Mr Morsell was alone and Carolus regretted this, for he had rather liked Beryl Morsell.

"My dear old chap," "Dear fellow," "My dear man" he distributed like largesse to the males in the bar and from Carolus asked heartily but not loudly how it was going.

"You haven't been to see me, dear old fellow," he said "I wish you'd come and have a natter over it. I'm full of ideas. Full of them. For instance, have you thought of those gardens?"

"Constantly," said Carolus. "They need *iris stylosa*."

"I don't think you can have realized their potentialities vis-à-vis the crime. No thanks. I daren't. Just a ginger ale. Example, you see."

From over his shoulder Carolus heard Doris.

"I should, Mr Lobbin. Just for a moment to see she's all right. Christmas evening and that. She surely won't

145

start again if you pop round there and speak nicely. You take my advice and nip in. It won't take you a second. If she starts again you can always fly back. Go on, now. Slip round there and get it over. She can't be as bad as you say, and if you hop in to show you've got over it, I'm sure it will be all right. Christmas-time."

Lobbin gave a preoccupied nod and picking up his overcoat left the bar.

16

THERE is something frightening about a sudden silence and tenseness falling on a room full of noisy people. Carolus believed afterwards that it came in the bar of the Queen Victoria hotel that evening before the re-entry of Lobbin as though in premonition of that. A babble was abruptly hushed, the last sound audible being the raucous laugh of Mrs Bullamy cut short.

Then there was Lobbin standing inside the door, his eyes staring vacantly out of a deathly white face.

" She's dead," he said loudly, yet to no one in particuar, " she has been murdered."

The silence continued for perhaps five seconds, before Mr Morsell rushed forward.

" Brandy, quick," he said and pushed Lobbin into a chair.

Carolus looked at his watch. It showed 8.27. Lobbin had been gone, he calculated, no more than five minutes.

Only three people in the room seemed to have the least idea what to do. Mr Morsell was in his element, telling people, quite unnecessarily, to stand back and give the man air, holding the brandy glass to his lips, saying 'feel better, old chap?' and generally taking charge of the situation.

Sitwell knew, too. He left the young woman with whom he had been sitting and went to the hall, evidently to telephone. This time there was to be no question about his efficiency when he had the luck to be first on the scene.

Carolus, if his conduct seemed callous, behaved at least consistently. Having noted the time he went up to Lobbin, ignoring Mr Morsell's protests, and said, " How had she been killed? "

Lobbin made a last attempt to concentrate before he lost what little of his senses were left to him.

" The hammer," he said, " the hammer from the shop." He did not speak again for a long time.

Then Carolus became more human. Looking over to the bar he saw that both Doris and Vivienne were gaping at Lobbin in a fixed and stupefied way and judged them to be very near hysteria.

"Doris," he said, then repeated it more loudly and peremptorily, " Doris! "

She tried to focus her attention on him.

" Do what I tell you, Doris. Pour out a whisky for me and a gin for yourself and one for Vivienne."

Doris's lip began to tremble.

" I couldn't," she said.

" Pour them out," insisted Carolus and rather falteringly she obeyed. " Now drink that! "

Doris's was the saddest ' Cheerio ' ever spoken. Vivienne drank too.

" I think I'm going to be sick," she said.

" No, you're not," Doris told her kindly. " Not in here, Vivienne. You swallow that and you'll feel better. D'you think it's true what he said, Mr Deene? "

Carolus might have replied that Lobbin was scarcely likely to be playing a practical joke but said, " We shall see. Just carry on as though nothing had happened, there's a good girl."

" Oh, isn't it awful, on Christmas night, and everything. What will happen, Mr Deene? "

" They'll take Lobbin away in a minute."

" Take him away? You mean lock him up? "

" Hospital, I expect," said Carolus. " Now will you

147

both be all right for a little while? I've got to go out but I'll be back as soon as I can."

Doris was still near tears, but nodded. " Don't be long," she said.

Carolus took the few paces to the door of Lobbin's shop. He saw that the shop itself was shut, but the door into the passage beside it, by which one entered the private part of the house, was still ajar. A light was on in the room above the shop.

He was about to enter when a police car drove up at speed and John Moore got out, followed by another plain clothes man.

" No, Carolus. I'm afraid not."

" Hullo, John. You got here quickly."

" Just as well I did."

He was through the door when Carolus said, " I've got a statement to make about this."

" Then come to my office presently. You can't come in here."

Carolus heard Moore's feet ascending the thinly carpeted stairs. Then he returned to the bar.

A small dispute was in progress between Mr Morsell and Sitwell.

" My orders are to take him round to the station to make a statement."

" And I say he's not in a condition to go."

" There's a police car waiting," said Sitwell.

" I don't care if there are a dozen. I am a minister of religion . . ."

" And I am a police officer. I intend to take this man to the police station."

" I shall not allow it."

" You would be obstructing the police in the execution of their duty."

" My duty is to a Higher Authority."

The argument was settled by Lobbin himself, who looked up wearily and said, " I'm quite willing to make a statement."

" I don't think you're in a condition . . ." began Mr Morsell.

" You heard what he said," retorted Sitwell and helped Lobbin to his feet.

" I shall insist on accompanying him," said Mr Morsell.

" You can do if you want," conceded the policeman. " There's plenty of room in the van."

The three went out.

This brought some easing of the general tension and Carolus's attention went to the young woman who had come in with Sitwell. He saw now that her hair and make-were in pronounced imitation of a certain film-star. She had an audience.

" Who'd be a copper's moll? " she asked. " Gone off without even paying for the drinks. Graham seems to have a nose for murder. It was he who discovered that other one a few weeks ago. And now this."

" He just happened to be here," said Mr Stringer sourly.

" He just happens to be wherever there's a murder," said the young woman with pride.

Carolus noticed that Doris was alone.

" Where's Vivienne? " he asked.

" Gone to phone her husband," Doris told him. " She thought he ought to know."

Doris was sufficiently recovered to have grown talkative.

" What a dreadful thing! " she said. " I shall never get over it, I'm sure. And his face, when he came in, did you ever see anything like it? Well, no wonder when you think of it. Finding her dead like that. It must have been horrible for him. Whoever can have done it, I wonder? Do you think it's the same as did the other one? He said something about a hammer, didn't he? Poor fellow, I do feel sorry for him. And only this evening they'd had one of their set-to's, so he told me. She shouting at him like I don't know what. It doesn't bear thinking about, does it? Vivienne was just as upset as I was, weren't you, Vivienne? "

" Mmmm," shuddered Vivienne, who had just returned.

149

"What did they want to take him away for? Mr Lobbin, I mean?"

"I expect they want a statement from him," said Carolus.

"You don't think they'd suppose he had anything to do with it, do you?"

"It depends on the evidence."

"But he can't have done. He was only gone a couple of minutes."

"A little more than five. He had the time to do it. That doesn't mean to say he did."

"I should think not! A nice fellow like Mr Lobbin. He wouldn't hurt a fly. It would have been small wonder if he'd done it long ago, the way she was always on to him. Anyone else might have but not him. He was far too good to her. You don't think they'd go and accuse him of it, do you?"

"Not unless they had very strong evidence of his guilt."

"That they couldn't have. He was in here all the time. Wasn't he, Vivienne?"

"Mmmm," said Vivienne with a suggestion of emphasis.

Carolus became aware that at the far end of the room Mr Biggett was standing and holding a glass of beer as though he feared it would be snatched away from him.

"How long has that little stout man been in here? The one by the street door?"

"Him? Oh he came in while you were out just now. He's been holding that glass of bitter ever since."

Carolus went to him.

"Good-evening," he said. "This is a break in your routine, isn't it?"

"Not at all," said Biggett. "On Christmas evening I always allow myself two half-pints of bitter. I have done so for the last twenty-three Christmases."

"Will you take your evening walk this evening?"

Biggett looked at him in amazement.

"Of course," he said. "Why not?"

"There has been another murder," Carolus pointed out.

" So I understand. It has nothing to do with my movements. I shall walk as usual."

Baulked of his chance to view the body, Carolus made the most of his observations in the bar. He consoled himself by thinking that the police would learn far more from the body than he would and that already their experts were at work, fixing the approximate time of the attack, collecting material for microscopic examination, carrying out their valuable routine scrutiny of the scene. His analyses were rarely based on such things though he was the last to undervalue them. He knew that although by some flash of insight, or from some haphazard sentence spoken by a suspect, he might be able to name the murderer, only the painstaking methods of the police could obtain the evidence needed to convict him. He was as likely to learn something here as from a visit to the room above the shop.

There were strangers in the room who seemed to behave in a somewhat subdued way though they were discussing the incident. Also there was Bodger, standing alone, and Mr and Mrs Bullamy talking together very earnestly. Mr Stringer seemed almost to be enjoying it as he went from group to group saying—" Terrible thing, isn't it? " and " Lucky the Reverend Morsell was here," and " You'd scarcely think it possible, would you? " Mr Rugley had entered, too, and was now standing quietly near the bar as though watching the interests of his business in this unusual crisis.

Then Carolus thought that in one way this case was unique in that he had stipulated and was to receive a large fee from the Rafter family. He considered that in view of this he would be expected to break the news to them. He decided to call on Bertrand first and then on Mrs Dalbinney, at whose flat he hoped to find both Emma and Paul. He could phone Locksley from one of these homes.

Bertrand opened the door himself and at once asked Carolus to come in.

" I'm delighted to see you," he said, but there was a

hint of interrogation in his voice, for it was little more than three hours since Carolus had left him.

" I've some news for you," said Carolus.

" Come on to the fire. I've opened a bottle of Cognac and am delighted to have someone to share it. It's a rather fine old Remy-Martin."

Yes, Bertrand would be a brandy man, thought Carolus, noting his host's velvet smoking jacket and Turkish slippers. He had noticed at lunch today that Bertrand's sense of quality in things was impeccable. Bertrand had nearly finished the cigar he was smoking and Carolus, who rarely smoked anything but cigars, badly wanted one. At last he pulled out his cigar case, only to find it empty.

" Have one of these," said Bertrand, though not with much enthusiasm. He opened a silver box of cigars of various kinds and handed it to Carolus. " No, not that. It's only half a cigar. Take one of these. Now what's your news? "

" Another murder," said Carolus, lighting up. " Lobbin's wife. With a hammer, it seems."

" Good heavens. When did this happen? "

" I don't know. It was discovered about half an hour ago." Carolus saw it was nine-thirty. " Yes, just an hour ago."

" Who discovered it? "

" Lobbin himself."

" He's not suspected, then? "

" I don't know. But I thought you ought to know about it. No one, after all, can begin talking of your family's motive this time."

" I see that. But I *am* sorry about it, Deene. She was a tiresome woman, I know, but it's dreadful for the poor fellow."

Carolus's eye fell on an open calf-bound book.

" What are you reading? " he asked.

" Gibbon. I'm not a historian like you, but when my dear Molly leaves me for an hour or two I usually devote the time to the Decline and Fall. Molly doesn't encourage serious reading," smiled Bertrand.

Carolus did not like leaving that cosy room and the warm electric fire, not to mention the brandy, but he said good-night to Bertrand and set off for Prince Albert Mansions.

This time the door was opened by Paul.

"We rather wondered if you'd come round," said Paul as he led him to where Mrs Dalbinney and Emma were sitting.

"Really? What made you think I might?"

Mrs Dalbinney answered.

"We are already informed," she said.

Carolus remembered Vivienne's phone call.

"The hall porter, I suppose?"

"The hall porter came up to tell us that Mrs Lobbin has been murdered in the same brutal way as . . ."

"No details are known yet," said Carolus sharply. "Lobbin has merely said that he found his wife dead."

"Is it true?" asked Emma quickly.

"I don't think Lobbin imagined it, naturally." Carolus spoke drily. "But at the same time we have very little information. The police are investigating now."

"She was a dreadful woman," said Mrs Dalbinney.

"And she has met a dreadful end."

"We are, of course, very sorry to hear about it, but at the same time it cannot affect us as the previous murder did. Not even the police could find any connection between our family and the murder of a newsagent's wife. You will not need to ask us questions this time, Mr Deene."

"No. I shan't. I came round to give you this news because I have been acting for you, but, as you suggest, this is a very different matter."

"Do you think the same person was responsible for both murders?" asked Emma.

"How can I possibly guess? I know nothing of the second murder yet."

"It was done with a hammer," Paul pointed out.

"So Lobbin said. He was dazed at the time. I may know a little more later when I have seen the police. But I don't think we should try to form any conclusions yet."

"Conclusions, no, but surely you must have some suspicions, Mr Deene?" said Mrs Dalbinney rather harshly. "You are an expert investigator and you have been devoting your time for some days to enquiries about a murder. Now another murder has been committed in the same town and—at least so it would appear—by the same or similar means. Are you without any opinion on these? When are we to hear who is guilty?"

"I am not without suspicions and if the facts are as we believe from Lobbin's remarks, I think there is only one murderer involved. But I'm not prepared to say any more at present."

"It is most unsatisfactory," pronounced Mrs Dalbinney. "Our family name . . ."

"Mrs Dalbinney," said Carolus with some exasperation. "A woman has been killed and whether or not he was the killer, one man at least is very near insanity this evening, I should judge. I don't think anyone is much concerned with your family or its name. I certainly cannot pretend that I am."

"You were employed to protect it."

"I was employed, as you put it, to find out who killed Ernest Rafter, and I have now every hope and intention of doing so."

"'Now'? Why 'now'?"

"Because very often, though it is a tragic truth, the only way to find the facts about one murder is through another one. In this case almost certainly."

"You mean you had to wait until this wretched woman was battered to death before you could discover who killed Ernest?"

"That is deliberately to misrepresent what I said. But let's not argue about it. I tell you only that *now* I believe I shall very soon know the whole truth. May I use your phone?"

Paul rose and led Carolus to a small room with a lot of books in it. A telephone was on the desk and Carolus was amused to see a large money-box beside it with a typewritten notice on it: 'Local Calls 3d. Please Ask Operator Cost of Others.'

He got through to Locksley Rafter at his home in Bawdon.

"Mr Rafter? This is Carolus Deene. I thought you ought to know that there has been another murder here in Selby."

"Already informed," the solicitor told him.

"Really? Then I needn't tell you that . . ."

"No thanks. Good night."

Carolus thoughtfully put a florin in the collecting-box and went back to Mrs Dalbinney.

"I didn't know you had telephoned your brother," he said.

"Of course. Immediately. He is not only my brother but my solicitor."

"Was he surprised at the news?"

"Not in the least. He has always suspected Lobbin."

"Ah yes. I remember he told me in that expansive way of his."

"My brother does not waste time or words," said Mrs Dalbinney.

"Or money, I hope," added Carolus impertinently.

"Certainly not."

"One other thing I would like to ask. Your brother Bertrand's secretary lives in this building, I believe."

This produced tension. Paul looked as though he wanted to laugh and Emma kept her eyes down.

"Or her parents do," amended Carolus. "Could you tell me the number?"

Mrs Dalbinney spoke as though she disliked doing so. "Do you know, Emma?"

"The second floor. Number 29," said Emma.

"Thank you."

Carolus realized that all three were looking at him inquisitively, wanting more information.

"I'll just look in," he said. "Her parents' name is French, I take it?"

This time Mrs Dalbinney was openly pained by the necessity to give information.

"Chigby," she said. "Mr and Mrs Chigby. French is the daughter's married name."

"I see. Thank you. Good-night," said Carolus.

The third and last door at which Carolus rang that night was not opened for several minutes. Then Molly French, wearing a coat and hat, appeared and said— "Darl . . . Oh, it's you. I was expecting Bertrand to call for me."

"Disappointing for you," said Carolus, then told her about the murder.

"I expect he's upset," said Molly, "that's why he didn't come. He should have been here at nine. My father and mother won't have the phone. Will you be an angel and run me back?"

"I'll certainly run you back," said Carolus, "though I can't promise to be an angel."

On that piece of fatuity they went downstairs and got in the car.

17

WHEN Carolus reached John Moore's office later that night he found John looking over-worked but alert, kept going by a strong brew of police-station tea. Carolus had known his friend to work through the night and was not surprised that he should be prepared to do so today.

"Thank heavens the wife hasn't joined me in Selby yet," he said, "she'd raise hell with me for keeping at it during Christmas. But what can I do? The preliminary reports are still coming in."

"Yes. It was an awkwardly timed murder from your point of view."

"You said you'd got something to report, Carolus. Do you mean that, or is it one of your fly-by-night theories?"

"I've certainly got no theory to put to you," said Carolus, "and I don't know how much use to you my little bits of information may be. But I'm quite willing to give you them."

"Go ahead, then."

"I was in the bar of the Queen Victoria when Lobbin came in at exactly 8.27 as I noticed. He had left the bar a few minutes earlier to go home and see his wife with whom he had quarrelled more violently than usual that evening. He was gone five to seven minutes by my reckoning."

Moore nodded, and Carolus went on to describe in detail Lobbin's appearance and behaviour in the bar, both before and after his dramatic announcement.

"The bar was crowded at the time," said Carolus, "mostly with people I did not know, but there were also a number I had met while I was mooning round making enquiries."

"Is that what you call it? Go on."

"Your policeman Sitwell came in with a very showy young woman."

"I know."

"And the parson who was on the promenade on the night of Ernest's murder was showing himself a good mixer with a glass of ginger ale."

Carolus described Mr Morsell's care of Lobbin.

"I know," said Moore again, "he came round here with him. I had quite a job to get rid of him. Officious type and I don't like all that 'old man' stuff."

"Bodger was in," said Carolus, "and a man called Stringer."

"How did you run into him?"

"He too was on the promenade that night, though I don't think Sitwell saw him. He spoke to Morsell, who is his Vicar."

"I know the man."

"Then there was a man called Biggett," said Carolus slyly, for he remembered that Moore had not yet traced the 'muffled-up' figure of the night of the murder. He thought that Moore was unlikely to admit this.

"Who?"

"Biggett. A Londoner who has recently come to live here. Retired."

"Do I know him?"

"I can't say. He's short and stout and walks about the promenade at night muffled up to the eyes."

Moore grinned.

"You mean?"

"Yes. I found him," said Carolus, "quite by luck, of course."

Carolus give Biggett's full name and address, which Moore wrote down.

"What is rather interesting about him is that he travelled down from London with Ernest Rafter that day. Ernest told him, quite frankly, that he was going to his family for money."

"How did you meet this man?"

"He continued his walks after the event, though avoiding Sitwell, I gather. He is a creature of habit." Carolus enlarged on this. "He always had two half-pints of beer on Christmas night and that, he said, was why he came to the Queen Victoria this evening. He arrived at the bar while I was outside Lobbin's shop waiting for you."

"Waiting for me! In another moment you'd have been up those stairs."

"At all events that is just when he arrived."

"It seems to have been quite a party in the bar. Anyone else?"

"The Bullamys, of course."

"Why, 'of course'?"

"They're in every evening."

"Are they? I admit I was rather interested in the Bullamys before this second murder. I've had a report on them from Australia. Somewhat shady characters. She did a short term of imprisonment some ten years ago. More recently they appeared to have come into or obtained a large sum of money and decided to 'retire', they said—though it was hard to know from what they were retiring. They gave out that they were going to live in England and here they are."

"Is there any evidence that they knew Rafter?"

"None, though they were in Brisbane at the same time. However, you say they were in the bar. Do you know what time they came in?"

"About eight, I think. That's their usual time. I noticed them talking to Lobbin once—nothing unusual about that. Earlier in the evening Emma Rafter came in for a quick drink, by the way. She often does."

Moore did not seem much interested in that. But he was appreciative of Carolus's information about the bar's customers that night.

"Very useful, Carolus. Any other bits and pieces you've picked up?"

"One or two. All connected with the first murder. I'm afraid you'll consider most of them irrelevant now. Though perhaps not the fact that Lobbin left the bar of the Queen Victoria for a short time on the night Ernest was killed. That night, as tonight, he had quarrelled with his wife. Apparently when he had had a drink he worried about it and when round to see her, but found her just as intractable and returned."

"I get the full point of that," said Moore.

"You know all about the scene between Mrs Dalbinney and Lobbin's wife?"

"Yes, I think so."

"And the movements of Emma Rafter and Isobel Dalbinney that night? They went for a breather on the promenade and saw Lobbin near the Palatine Cinema at soon after ten."

"Yes. I know about that."

"Morsell's finding the public lavatory closed . . ."

"No. What's that?"

Carolus told him and went on to the Bullamys and the man they saw crossing the road.

"They came and told me that. But only a few days ago. They did not mention it when I first saw them."

"I think I scared them into coming to you. Then I

take it Locksley Rafter has told you of his movements that night?'

"Oh yes. He seemed to want to convince me that he had been quite near the shelter at the time of the murder."

"Curious, isn't it? The only other thing I have to tell you is that Ernest Rafter had an envelope full of treasury notes in his breast pocket that night. Did you know that?"

"I did not actually know he had it on him, but I knew he received an envelope with money in it. His King's Cross landlady says that the only letter he received during his two weeks with her contained money, because he immediately pulled out some notes and paid her. Unfortunately it was not registered or we could have traced the sender."

"And it was not found on the body?"

"No envelope containing money. Seven pounds in a pocket case in his hip pocket."

"So robbery could have been the motive?"

"It could, I suppose. Or one of the motives."

"Or the money could have been removed to suggest robbery?"

"That, too."

"Or the corpse could have been rifled by someone other than the murderer?"

"I suppose that can't be ruled out."

"Look, John. You're putting on your old air of inscrutability. Do you think you know who killed Ernest Rafter?"

"I can't answer that just now, Carolus."

"And Bella Lobbin?"

"I'm holding her husband.'

"Have you sufficient evidence for that?"

"Enough to charge him. I can't do anything else."

"I'd like to know your case, as it stands."

"First of all it's a matter of common sense. Unless you want me to believe that there are two murderers in this town."

"I don't want you to believe anything."

"It all boils down to motive, Carolus. As usual. Tell me who else in the word had motives for murdering both these people? Lobbin has made a statement in which he admits recognizing Ernest Rafter as a collaborator of the Japanese, who helped to make his life, and that of other prisoners, a greater hell than it already was. He denies having spoken to him, but says he saw him in the bar of the Queen Victoria that night and, although at first he was uncertain, he was afterwards quite sure of his man. I conclude that since you say Ernest had a wad of money on him Lobbin could have seen him pull it out in the Queen Victoria. So even if it was robbery . . ."

"Other people could have seen that. The barmaid in fact did see it and I daresay the Bullamys could have done so."

"As I've told you, I don't think the principal motive was robbery. The very way in which the murder was done argues a maniacal hatred."

"Or a maniacal something-or-other."

"I think Lobbin recognized Ernest, heard him say he was going to the promenade, went home and got his weapon . . ."

"But he still had a coal-hammer in his shop afterwards."

"He could have had two, surely? Followed him down to the promenade, murdered and robbed him. I am driven to this conclusion because no one else had motive *and* opportunity."

"So far as we know.'

"Then the second murder. The side door of the house had not been forced. Only Lobbin and his wife had keys."

"I'm not necessarily disagreeing with you, John, but I think it may be helpful to point out snags. Mrs Lobbin could have opened the door to the murderer if it wasn't Lobbin."

"She could have. But wait. We come to motive once again. Tell me who else in the world could have a motive for killing that woman? Lobbin had suffered from her tongue for twenty years. He made no secret of the kind of hell she made his life. She had killed his (perhaps silly, but to him very real) ambition to write. There is an end to everyone's patience and I think he reached his tonight."

"You haven't convinced me yet. And I don't believe you're quite convinced yourself."

"I haven't had detailed reports yet, but I do know that the only fingerprints found in the room are those of Lobbin and his wife. Moreover the hammer used belonged to them."

"It had been lying in the shop for some days. Bella Lobbin kept it as an exhibit to show it had not been used to murder Ernest. Anyone could have seen it there."

"But the street door of the shop was locked. Did Bella Lobbin allow this mysterious murderer of yours to go down from the rooms above the shop to fetch the hammer with which to kill her? Who else could have got it *but* her husband?"

"Circumstantial," said Carolus annoyingly.

"Then time. On a first examination the police surgeon, who reached the place at half past nine, an hour after Lobbin claims to have found his wife dead, thinks death occurred between one and three hours before he saw the body. So Lobbin could either have killed her before going to the pub and then gone back to 'find' her dead, or during the seven minutes while he was absent. At all events it seems, again on a preliminary examination, that this time the blows were unmistakably the work of a powerful man. In the other case the hammer was heavier and could have been used by almost anyone. This time a man of Lobbin's build is strongly suggested."

"What does Lobbin himself say to all this?"

"Denies it, of course. But can't suggest anyone else who might have a motive for killing his wife."

"I should like to be the barrister defending him. I don't think you have a chance of convicting him on what you've told me."

"But you take no account of the experts' evidence.

That is all to come. I shall be surprised if it isn't conclusive."

"If it is, I shall have nothing more to say. I'm the last to under-rate the importance of expert evidence in a case like this. I've got nothing to show against it. But I'm going to ask you one thing, John, in return for what I've been able to tell you tonight. It's all-important to me. Will you let me know whether your experts agree on one point? That Bella Lobbin was killed by the hammer found beside her; that is, the hammer from the shop?"

"You want to introduce a new hammer?"

"Not necessarily. But I do want an answer to that. It can be no breach of confidence, because that evidence would have to come out in Court afterwards. If it wasn't, if some other weapon was used, I may have something worth putting to you. If it was, my notions are probably wrong."

"I'll remember your request," said Moore guardedly.

"One other thing. Was anyone else seen approaching Lobbin's shop this evening?"

"That's a foolish question, Carolus. It's a busy little street. Even if anyone had been watching it all the evening they could only say that a number of people had passed. Most of those you observed in the pub for instance."

"And was anyone watching?"

"Not that I know of. There's a woman who keeps the sweetshop opposite whom I questioned this evening, but she says she saw nothing, never looked out of her window, heard nothing, knows nothing and wouldn't tell us anyway if she did. She was prosecuted for selling short weight some months ago and has a violent hatred for the police. But I gained the impression she really didn't see anything, even Lobbin's going out or return. You can try her, if you like. Mrs Cocking, her name is. I wish you luck with her."

"Thanks. I will."

"I don't know what you're up to, Carolus, or what

wonderfully abstruse theory you are going to pull out of your hat, but you can't get away from motive. It's the key which opens everything. Only one man, as I have told you, had the opportunity and motive in the first murder. Only one man had opportunity and motive in the second murder. And *it's the same man*. What more do you want? "

" Evidence," said Carolus.

" We'll get that tomorrow when our reports come in. Even bloodstains."

" What bloodstains? "

" On Lobbin's overcoat. When he returned to the pub."

" Presumably he made sure that his wife was dead."

" There wasn't much need for that," said Moore.

" Still, it's not extraordinary that someone who discovers a corpse in that condition should afterwards find that somehow or other . . ."

" All right, Carolus. Only you talked about evidence. That's the sort of evidence a jury wants. They love bloodstains."

" Are we talking about the same thing? I want to find the truth. You seem to be interested chiefly in a conviction."

" That's not fair, Carolus.

" Perhaps not. But you can't help being a policeman, John. I don't mean by that that you'd try to get a man hanged unless you were convinced. Only you naturally want to tidy up every case you handle with a conviction. It's your job. However, it's past one o'clock and I suppose you mean to be up bright and early."

John Moore detained him a few minutes longer, however.

" You said just now you might have what you called something worth putting to me. Does that mean you have a theory? "

" The beginnings of what may become one."

" Does it cover both the crimes? "

Carolus seemed to consider this before answering.

" Yes," he said at last. " It does. At least it will if it

164

comes to be tenable. At present it seems too fantastic, even to me."

"Does it involve Lobbin?"

"I think you would be wise to hold Lobbin."

"When are you going to put it to me?"

"That depends on your answer to my question about the hammer. Good-night, John."

When he reached the Queen Victoria hotel he had to ring for a long time before a very sleepy George opened the door. But the porter's manner, even at this hour, remained foxy and rather ingratiating.

"There's been someone on the phone for you," he said. "Wants you to call as soon as you come in."

"Did he give his name?"

"Yes. Grainger or Gorilla or something. The number's Newminster 9966."

"Gorringer," said Carolus absently. "As soon as I came in?"

"It was only about ten when he rung. I expect he's asleep by now," said George.

"I shall faithfully carry out his request," said Carolus and went to the phone-box.

Mr Gorringer was one of those people who think it necessary to shout on the telephone, as though the thing were still in its infancy. It took him some minutes to answer and when he did so the ear-piece rattled.

"Deene? But it is one-thirty a.m.!"

"You asked me to call you," said Carolus innocently.

"I had no idea you would disturb me in the small hours of the morning. However, since you have done so, I must tell you that I have received a call from Mrs Dalbinney. She tells me that so far from easing the anxieties of herself and her family, you have spent your time asking them irrelevant questions while another murder has been committed."

"Another what?" asked Carolus mischievously.

"Murder!" bellowed Mr Gorringer, then aside—"No, no, my dear. I was talking to Deene."

"Didn't she say it lets her out?" asked Carolus.

" Your words are meaningless to me. The fact is that one of our most respected parents is distressed by your conduct. And by the course of events."

" She needn't be. She's a silly self-important woman . . ."

" I must ask you not to speak in that way of one of the most valued of the school's supporters. I feel, in the circumstances, that my presence in Selby-on-Sea is highly advisable. Further complications must be avoided at all costs."

" Do you mean another murder? "

" I am speaking of the unfortunate *tracasserie* which seems to have broken out between you and Mrs Dalbinney. My modest gift for pouring oil on troubled waters seems urgently in demand. I shall make the journey tomorrow."

" Just as you like, headmaster. How will you come? "

" Hm, I am informed by Hollingbourne that he has purchased a small but reliable motorcar. You may expect me towards lunchtime."

" I shall be in the bar of the Queen Victoria," said Carolus. " Are you bringing your wife? "

" Mrs Gorringer has other engagements of a more congenial character."

" You'll just arrive for the kill," said Carolus.

" The *what*? " shouted Mr Gorringer in horror.

" The *dénouement*," said Carolus.

" *Eh bien. A demain, alors*," said the headmaster, to whom a piece of anglicized French was always a challenge.

18

AT ten o'clock next morning Carolus stood outside Mrs Cocking's shop and wondered at its survival, a sweetshop of the old kind. So you could still buy liquorice sprinkled with hundreds and thousands? And great sticky bullseyes and coloured fruit drops? He would have thought the modern child had lost its taste for such simple pleasures.

Mrs Cocking was diminutive but solid, like a stumpy thick piece of the Selby Rock she sold. A faint dark moustache, a husky voice and a pair of short muscular fore-arms were all noticeable to Carolus.

" Good morning," he said bravely. " Could I have half a pound of sugared almonds please? "

Mrs Cocking examined him with a scowl but did not move to fulfil his order.

" *You* don't want sugared almonds," she said with un-concealed hostility.

" As a matter of fact I don't," said Carolus cheerfully, forgetting her reason for resentment.

Mrs Cocking's form of attack was interrogatory.

" I knew it. As soon as you walked in the shop I knew what you was after. Thought you were going to make another fine out of me, didn't you? Got your little scales and measures all ready, haven't you? Waiting to say there was one sugared almond short, weren't you? Nasty creeping snooper, aren't you? Well, you can take yourself off out of here. I'm not serving you."

" I'm not interested in weights and measures," said Carolus.

" What is it this time, then? Going to say I sold a bar of chocolate after hours, are you? Thought you'd scare me into saying anything that suited you, did you? Want to have me up in Court while you swear on the Bible I've broken the law, do you? You can try those tricks on someone else."

" Mrs Cocking, I am not a policeman or an inspector of any kind. I dislike them quite as much as you do."

Mrs Cocking gave a loud grunt.

" Then what did you come here for, asking for sugared almonds which you didn't want? Answer me that."

" I came to ask you for some information."

" Oh so that's it. You think I'm going to grass some other poor soul who happens to have a set of scales that wants seeing to? You think I'm going to help get some-one else in trouble, do you? All to help the police, do you? "

"On the contrary, if you have the information I want it will not help the police at all. They won't be pleased, in fact."

"Oh," said Mrs Cocking, still on the defensive but more interested.

"They intend to charge Lobbin with the murder of his wife," said Carolus.

"Just like them!" said Mrs Cocking. "After the way that bitch screeched and yelled at him all day till he didn't know what he was doing. He ought to have a medal for it, if you ask me. And the police have locked him up for it, have they?"

Carolus smiled patiently.

"It's not a question of whether or not Lobbin had provocation, but whether or not he murdered his wife. The police think he did."

"They would!" said Mrs Cocking darkly. "They'd think anything if it suited them."

"I don't believe he did," said Carolus and waited for the effect.

"You don't? Well, I must say I hadn't thought . . ."

"You took it for granted the police were right?"

"Right? I wouldn't demean myself by thinking about them."

"But over Lobbin?"

"Well, I mean to say, the way she's gone on at him."

"Mrs Cocking, may I explain that I think there is the gravest doubt as to whether Lobbin killed his wife. It could have been someone different."

It was clear that Mrs Cocking would have been glad to incline to this theory but found it difficult to adopt.

"Of course if you say so," she said dubiously.

"It depends very largely on you."

"Me? How do I come into it?"

"You told the police you had seen nothing last night."

"I should think I did! I told them more than that. I told them not to let me catch them crawling round here again. Always trying to get someone in trouble."

" And not always the right person."

" Right person! What do you mean? Could I help it if my scales wanted seeing to? "

" I was thinking about the murder."

" Oh that. Well it had to come some day. I've said so a hundred times."

" Mrs Cocking, when you told the police you had seen nothing last night you were helping them to convict Lobbin."

This seemed at last to go home.

" I wouldn't do that, poor fellow," said Mrs Cocking. " He's had enough to put up with as it is without being hanged on the top of it."

" Then will you try to think back to last night? "

" I don't need to think back to it. I remember it all perfectly well."

" You were watching? "

" As it happens I was just taking a peep to see everything was all right before I went to bed. I'd heard them on at one another earlier, but that was nothing unusual. We're accustomed to that in this street. It's a pity there's not a china shop because it would have done a roaring trade with them every time she started on the smash. So I saw this person go to the door . . ."

" What person? " asked Carolus breathlessly.

" How am I to know what person? I couldn't see his face, if it *was* a he. Grey overcoat he wore."

" Why do you say ' if it was a he '? "

" Well, you never know, do you? "

" Yes," said Carolus. " So you saw this person go to the door? "

" And her come down and let him in."

" Had you ever seen him before? "

" Not that I know of but I couldn't see his face. I thought to myself, hullo, I thought, that must be the doctor going to see her to calm her down a bit."

" How long was he with her? "

" Well, I didn't actually see him go because I was making myself a cup of cocoa. I heard the door opposite slam and went to see but it was too late. He must have gone."

"You heard nothing while he was in there?"

"You can't hear anything from across here," said Mrs Cocking regretfully, "unless it was when she started on at him, then the whole street could hear it."

"If that slam was Lobbin's side-door . . ."

"Well it was. I'm sure of that. I know the way the knocker rattles when it's slammed."

"If that meant the departure of Mrs Lobbin's visitor, how long do you think he was in there?"

"Ten minutes, I daresay. So near as I could tell."

"Did you see Lobbin come back?"

"Yes. About a quarter of an hour later. Let himself in. It didn't take him long to do for her . . ."

"Mrs Cocking, I don't believe he killed his wife."

"You can believe what you like. You've never heard how she got on to him."

"Why are you so sure? Couldn't it have been the man you saw go in first?"

"What, the doctor? What would he want to do for her for?"

Incorrigible, thought Carolus, but he had the information he had scarcely hoped for.

"You're quite sure of your facts, Mrs Cocking?"

"Of course I am. And I only hope they help to get him off. After all, it was more than half an accident, I daresay, and after the way she shouted at him he couldn't hardly have been in his right mind. So along come the police and lock him up and accuse him of this that and the other. I'm sure if there's anything I can say to help him, I'll say it. They can't do anything to me for Speaking, can they?"

Carolus returned to the Queen Victoria to await Mr Gorringer. Until John Moore gave him the information he wanted there was nothing he could do, and he prepared to receive the headmaster with the friendly amusement he always felt for him. But even Carolus could scarcely have anticipated Mr Gorringer's appearance as it presently manifested itself.

The headmaster wore a large cloth cap, the peak of which came halfway down his forehead. Dark glasses concealed his protuberant eyes and the collar of his overcoat was turned up, though it could not hide his huge hairy ears by which Carolus would have immediately recognized him, even if the whole disguise had been more effective.

"I want you to understand, my dear Deene, that I am strictly incognito here."

"Yes. You look it," said Carolus. "Where on earth did you get that cap, headmaster?"

"Not 'headmaster', please, Deene. The title must be forgotten for the duration of my stay. I do not wish the fair name of the Queen's School to be bandied about. Now please tell me how matters stand in this deplorable case."

"They don't," said Carolus. "I'm not certain they ever will. The police are charging the husband of the murdered woman with the second crime."

"That sounds logical," said Mr Gorringer.

"To other married men perhaps," said Carolus, remembering Mrs Gorringer's witticisms, "but not to me."

"Are you proposing once again to vaunt your private opinion in opposition to the results of scrupulous and patient research by the police force?"

"Not yet. I've got very little really with which to oppose anyone. I begin to see a possibility but it is vague and fantastic. 'I see men as trees walking'."

"In that case, Deene, would it not be the properly modest thing to leave the whole matter to the discretion of those more experienced in practical criminology? I cannot but think that your tendency to opinionativeness smacks of arrogance."

"Can't do that," said Carolus. "I've got my obligations to the Rafter family, apart from a sense of justice."

"But the Rafter family, I gather, would be only too glad to accept the police solution."

"I don't think so, if they thought it meant hanging the wrong man."

"Oh come now. Do not let us use such violent terms."

"Hanging is a violent business. So is murder, very often."

Carolus became aware that Doris was calling him into conference.

"I say!" she said. "Whoever's that? *He* looks as though he might be the murderer any day. Wherever did you find him?"

"An old acquaintance of mine."

"The police have still got poor Mr Lobbin. Do you think they're going to try and hang him? I don't believe he did it and never shall, whatever the police say about it. He's far too much of a gentleman to go banging anyone on the head with a coal-hammer. *You* don't think he did it, do you, Mr Deene?"

"The police have certainly got a case against him. It's hard to see, if he didn't murder his wife, who else had any reason to do so."

"Anyone might," said Doris with generous exaggeration. "The kind of woman she was. You never know. There's more than one must have felt like it before now."

Carolus returned to the headmaster, who had evidently been studying the quiet mid-day customers with some attention.

"I should be interested to know," he said in a low voice to Carolus, "whether any of your suspects are present? I sense something sinister in the atmosphere of this bar, Deene, and as you know my instincts are keen in such matters."

"No, I don't think anyone here has been thought of in connection with the murders, though in a sense the whole town is suspect."

"Indeed? A wide net, Deene, a wide net."

Carolus noted that the headmaster had drawn from his pocket a large pipe of the shape usually associated with Baker Street. This he now proceeded to fill and light.

" My chief preoccupation," he said, " is the continuing goodwill of Mrs Dalbinney. I intend to call on her this afternoon. What reassurance may I take to her from you? "

" Tell her she's not a suspect."

The headmaster managed a grudging smile.

" You were ever addicted to flippancy," he said. " By what wild flight of the imagination could it ever be supposed that Mrs Dalbinney, a member of a distinguished family, the mother of two sons educated at the Queen's School, Newminster, a lady whom I have considered inviting to distribute the prizes on the occasion of our next Speech Day, that such a person should slay her fellow human beings with a hammer intended for coal-breaking? "

" One of the noteworthy points about the first murder was that a child could have done it. It needed no particular strength of arm."

" Ah Deene, Deene," the headmaster chuckled pointedly. " There are times when your sense of humour is sadly wanting. The absurdity of even considering Mrs Dalbinney did not lie in any physical disability. But let be. As Mrs Gorringer once said, with her clever sense of *plaisanterie* and *apropos*, there are times when one is tempted to speak of you as the Gloomy Deene. But to return to our *moutons*. What shall I tell Mrs Dalbinney when I see her? "

" Oh nothing from me. I don't know yet whether I shall ever have a strong enough case even to put forward, and if I have it will be useless unless I can persuade the Detective Inspector in charge that it is worth a try."

" What do you mean by a try, may I venture to enquire? "

" A search for supporting evidence. Of that I can promise none. But if the police are satisfied that there may be reason for it, they will find that fast enough."

" In those circumstance your task will have been fulfilled? "

" Yes."

" Anonymously, I take it? "

" Of course."

" In that case you would scarcely have any claim on the good nature of the members of the Rafter family, and certainly none on their pockets."

" On the contrary, I should put in my bill at once."

Just then Locksley Rafter entered. Carolus had never seen him in this bar before and Doris, as Carolus discovered later, was unacquainted with him. He joined Carolus, who introduced him to ' Mr Hugh Gorringer, headmaster of the Queen's School, Newminster '.

" Nay, Deene," said Mr Gorringer, " As I have told you I am travelling incognito. I am a simple citizen for the nonce."

" Queen's School myself," said Locksley unexpectedly. " Before your time."

Mr Gorringer, who found it hard to recognize that there had been a Queen's School before his time, said, " Ah yes. Very likely. You'd find a great many changes now. Numbers have trebled since I took up the reins of office."

" Quality, in my time," said Locksley curtly, leaving Mr Gorringer somewhat baffled.

Carolus relieved the slight tension.

" Do you know," he asked Locksley, " whether on the night your brother was killed a phone call was received at your house? "

" It was," said Locksley.

" From whom? "

" Identity unknown."

" Male? "

" Yes."

" What did the caller want? "

" To speak to me."

" Did he give any indication at all of his identity? "

" Yes. A relative."

" Anything else? "

" He had tried the others. No reply."

174

"By the others presumably he meant your brother and sisters?"

"Presumably."

"You did not tell me this when I saw you."

"No. You made no enquiry."

"It was of some considerable importance. We knew that Ernest had been to the telephone but did not know whether he had spoken to anyone. Who took the call?"

"My wife."

"Did she make any conjecture about it at the time?"

"Probably. Women are given to conjecture."

"Did she know of Ernest?"

"No."

"Not even that such a person had existed?"

"Nothing."

Locksley left them and Mr Gorringer approached the bar with the intention, it seemed, of inviting Carolus to have a drink. Carolus followed closely.

"Can I persuade you?" Mr Gorringer asked Carolus tentatively.

"Thanks. I'll have another Scotch."

"And for me a Guinness," said the headmaster. "I wonder whether this modest hotel of yours provides a good luncheon, Deene? I begin to feel that some reinforcement would not be amiss."

"There's stewed rabbit today," said Doris. "It's ever so nice the way cook does it with pearl barley."

"Simple fare," commented the headmaster, "but not unpalatable, I think. What say you, Deene?"

But before they went to try it, Carolus was called into the hall of the hotel by Mr Rugley. He found John Moore waiting for him impatiently.

"You were right, Carolus," he said at once. "Bella Lobbin was not killed with the hammer that was beside her. A much smaller and lighter one was used for the actual blows. The one I found had been placed there and blooded on purpose."

"Thank God," said Carolus.

" Why? What exactly are you going to argue from this? "

" It means that Lobbin did not do it."

" It suggests that he did not. It does not make it certain."

" There is no certainty in this case. I saw Mrs Cocking, by the way. She talked."

" Yes? "

" She saw someone go to Lobbin's last night and be admitted by Bella while Lobbin was out."

" She wouldn't tell me that," said Moore.

" She wouldn't tell you anything. She doesn't like policemen."

" Do you know who it was Bella Lobbin let into her house last night? "

" I think so."

" The murderer? "

" I think so."

" You'd better give me the full results of all this thinking, then," said Moore impatiently.

" I will. But I want to go over some notes first and get ideas straightened out."

" All very nice. But as usual you fail to appreciate our practical difficulties. I can't hold Lobbin much longer."

" Come round here at six this evening if you like."

" Not earlier? "

" No. I should like to let Gorringer be here. It does give the old boy such pleasure to be ' in on the ground floor ' as he calls it."

" I've no objection except that you seem to be treating the whole thing rather lightly."

" I'm not, John. I can't help being a facetious creature, but I never take murder lightly and certainly not these murders."

Moore looked at him curiously.

" I should have thought these . . . after all one was a collaborator and the other a scold. Not people to arouse one's quickest sympathy."

"It's not a question of sympathy. I'm not thinking of the victims. However, you shall hear what I think this evening."

19

"LET me say at once," began Carolus when the three of them were sitting in a small room which Mr Rugley had provided for them, "let me say at once that I have never had so little to offer. There's scarcely a scrap of real evidence in the lot of it, and all I can do is to put forward a possibility, a fantastic and gruesome possibility, and leave it to you, John, to decide whether you think it's worth examination. If you put your whole resources into it you will, I believe, find the proof you want, but in the meantime I can do no more than sketch a crazy outline.

"I come to it by that most dangerous of ways of thinking in matters of crime—the improbability of all others. When I first began to meet the people connected with the case, who for want of a better word we may call suspects, I found it flatly incredible that any of them could have murdered Ernest Rafter for the motives attributed to them. Apart from other forms of improbability, could one conceive of any of the members of that highly respectable family caring so much about the return of Ernest from the dead that one of them would waylay him in a lonely shelter and smash his skull in with a hammer? And that, even if any of them, apart from Emma, knew that he was alive, or if any of them at all knew that he had come to Selby? They were, it has been suggested, somewhat avaricious or pettily mean in different ways, but could you conceive of one of them in his senses wishing to murder Ernest rather than pay him out with a probably quite modest sum of money? It was unthinkable and, as Bertrand pointed out to me, anyone could have foreseen that the murder of Ernest would bring wide and unpleasant publicity for the family, as indeed it did.

"No, family pride or family avarice as a motive for murdering Ernest simply could not be considered seriously and when I came to the other so-called motives I found the same thing. Revenge as a motive for murder has always seemed highly suspect to me even when it is revenge for some specific injury suffered. Revenge, in a general sort of retributory way for what a man may or may not have done to his fellows twenty years ago, is more unbelievable still. As soon as I talked to Lobbin and Bodger, both of whom were supposed to come under suspicion because they had particular reasons for hating collaborators of the Japanese, I was convinced that whatever their feelings had been or were they did not provide a motive for a particular murder.

"I looked for other possible motives and of course robbery had to be considered. I knew from Doris that Ernest had a roll of notes in an envelope in his breast-pocket while he was in the bar that evening, and I knew that it was not on the corpse when it was found. Doris assured me that he had only pulled it out once that evening, that almost certainly no one except herself and perhaps Vivienne had seen it, but I could not know this for certain. It was just possible that someone in the bar of the Queen Victoria had seen that Ernest had money on him and so had armed himself with a coal-hammer, followed Ernest down to the promenade and killed him for the sake of it. Or that someone (like Mr Biggett for example), who was not in the bar that night, knew of it and did the same. Or that some thug who knew nothing of Ernest was lying in wait near the last shelter to murder and rob the first person who came to it.

"But honestly—look at the improbabilities involved here. There was no one 'out of the ordinary' in the bar that night and can one reasonably suspect the quiet folk who frequent the place of carrying out such a brutal and dangerous crime for the sake of a roll of notes of unknown value? Or can one make oneself believe in some mysterious stranger following Ernest from London because of this modest sum and, *guessing* that he would go to the last shelter, waiting there for him? Or can one really suppose there was an unknown thug with a weapon ready? In any of these cases one must remember, too, that Ernest could probably have been robbed fairly easily without the extraordinary violence of the attack. So I did *not* believe in robbery as a motive.

"That left me with a huge question mark, not who had killed Ernest, but *why had he been killed*. If I could answer that the rest would be easy. Not family pride or avarice, not revenge, not robbery. What was left? Only, it began to seem to me, one thing—madness. A murder without a motive. A murder for the lust of killing. Or a murder for some abstruse psychopathic satisfaction which I could not follow.

"At first it seemed monstrous and as improbable, almost, as the other explanations, but as I thought about it I saw that it accounted for several things which were otherwise unaccountable. I began to work on it as a macabre but increasingly attractive hypothesis.

"Suppose someone, man or woman, wanted to commit a murder merely for the sake of it. It might be a perfectly normal human being outwardly, a respected citizen, a good father or mother, someone undistinguished from his fellows except by this single schizophrenic craving which was kept secret. Suppose such a person was looking for a place in which to carry out his intention—where better could he find than the deserted promenade of a small seaside town in winter? And on that promenade, where better than the last shelter, visited only occasionally by the hardiest exercise-takers?

"My monster was beginning to become real to me, though I could not yet decide with certainty on the sex. I imagined him visiting the shelter from time to time— not often enough to attract attention—always armed with the weapon he had most intelligently chosen, an old well-used hammer which he may have kept for the purpose for years. His idea was to wait till the circumstances com-

179

bined in his favour, then commit his murder and walk away as carelessly as he pleased, secure that even if seen no one would suspect him, for he had no motive. He could wait as long as he pleased for the right occasion, for a great deal of his satisfaction, I thought, was in anticipation.

" He did not have to wait for some particular kind of victim, if I was right, for this was not a sexual thing or a piece of sadism. It was a calculated wish to have killed a human being, nothing more nor less. So the murderer could pick the first arrival when the circumstances were propitious.

" At first I knew very little about him or her. I could not guess whether he was a resident of long standing or a new arrival, whether he was one of those seen on the promenade that night or not, whether he was young or old, male or female, a respected person or a tramp; I only knew that he had probably spied out the land long before that evening and laid his plans very carefully.

" That was one of the things that had mystified me most about the murder of Ernest Rafter. It was a planned murder, that was certain. The place chosen, the weapon carried, everything suggested long and careful planning. Yet no one seemed to have known that Ernest was still alive, let alone that he was coming to Selby on a certain night and would walk on the promenade late and choose that particular shelter. The only conclusion I could draw from this was that the murder had been planned *without a particular victim in mind.*

" There was one possible alternative to this—that Ernest had been murdered in mistake for someone else. But I dismissed this again on the grounds of improbability. There was enough light in the last shelter, in fact, to make it more than unlikely. So I began to sketch out a picture of an unknown murderer waiting of an evening in a special place for an unknown and unimportant victim.

" But the details of the picture entirely eluded me. If, as I conjectured, it was someone who showed no sign of abnormality in ordinary life it could have been almost anyone we knew was on the promenade that night—Lobbin, Bodger, Biggett, Stringer, Paul or even Sitwell himself. Or it could have been one of the married people who were there in pairs, the Morsells or the Bullamys. But it could also have been someone who was not seen at all, or who was briefly seen but not recognized, like the man crossing the road. It could have been someone who came from the public garden or someone who came from the beach, it could have been someone seen walking away or someone who afterwards remained hidden in the garden or on the beach . . ."

"No," interrupted John Moore. "Those were searched, of course."

"Some time later. Indeed, so little was known of my hypothetic murderer-for-the-sake-of-it that I remember thinking he would never be discovered. He had calculated that a murder without motive was a murder for which no one would ever be hanged, and it looked as if he was right.

"Yet I believed in him, for, fantastic though the thing was, he made the very people whom I had dismissed because their motives were incredible suspects again. That Bodger would not have killed Ernest because his son had died on the Burma road seemed certain to me, but I could not be sure that Bodger was not secretly a madman determined to kill the first human being conveniently in a certain place at night. The same applied to Lobbin. And with some of the others, like Morsell, for instance, and Bullamy it actually provided—if not a motive in the strict sense of the word, at least a madman's reason for the thing. It made the whole town suspect."

Mr Gorringer raised his hand to halt the argument. Clearly he wished to pronounce.

"It is time, I feel, that we refreshed ourselves. The ingenious Deene is apt to be carried away by his theories and we are left—high and dry, may I say? Inspector, may I suggest a drink?"

Carolus rang a bell beside him and George appeared.

While he was bringing the drinks they had ordered, Mr Gorringer expressed his approval of Carolus's wild theorizing.

"Though, as you yourself admit, my dear Deene, your notions have elements of the *fantastique*, I must say I like them. The case itself is not without fantasy and you have matched it. *No* motive, eh? That is indeed something new. It certainly seems to have rendered detection exactingly complicated. Do you argue then that if I, for example, were to walk out into the night and murder the first stranger I met I should remain undetected?"

"Probably. Unless you were caught *in flagrante delicto*."

"Curious," said the headmaster. "Highly curious. I had not considered it before. But in this case it seems to have hard logic behind it. And what I particularly like is the fact that your theory (if you substantiate it) instantly disposes of one of the most undesirable and ridiculous features of this case—the absurd suspicions which have attached themselves to members of the Rafter family."

"Why?" asked Carolus.

"I beg your pardon?" said Mr Gorringer, who was taken aback by this interrogative monosyllable.

"Why does it dispose of the Rafters?"

"Surely you must see, my dear Deene, that the only thing (and that in my mind an *ignis fatuus*) which could be held to connect even remotely with the crime these highly respected citizens, was that they were supposed to have something accounted a motive for wishing to dispose of Ernest. If you show that such a motive (or pretence at one) had nothing to do with the murder, you at once show that *they* had nothing to do with it. Not that such a demonstration was necessary."

"I still say: 'Why?'. Why are the Rafters not as suspect as anyone else?"

"I find the question little short of obtuse," said the headmaster huffily. "Are you going to suggest that one of them would have carried this morbid craving for causing death to the length of murdering his own brother?"

"Or uncle," added Carolus. "But I didn't say that. I asked why you thought they were excluded from suspicion. You seem to forget that if, as they all claim, they did not know that Ernest was in Selby that night and had not seen him for twenty years, they would not have known who it was sitting in that corner of the shelter. They are no more exempt from suspicion than anyone else."

"Fiddlesticks," said Mr Gorringer.

"As a matter of fact," continued Carolus unshaken, "if I am proved right it was one of the family who murdered Ernest."

"I take it this is more of your ill-chosen facetiousness," said the headmaster severely. "Or are you going to tell me that Mrs Dalbinney stalked along the promenade with a coal-hammer with which to murder the first person she might meet?"

"No. It was Bertrand," said Carolus.

20

MR GORRINGER affected to laugh.

"So you ask the Inspector and me to suppose that Lieutenant-Colonel Bertrand Rafter, who was awarded the MBE during the last war, a man of the highest integrity, was responsible for the murder of his brother?"

He smiled towards John Moore as if to draw him into his own attitude of disdain for such silliness, but saw that Moore was listening attentively.

"Responsible is not the word I should have chosen," said Carolus. "Part of him at least is barking mad."

"I see. Dr Jekyll and Mr Hyde."

"Not so clear-cut. But something of the sort."

"Let's have it, Carolus," said Moore.

"I first suspected Bertrand when he knew that Ernest had been robbed. Who else could know that except the murderer? The police had no idea of it. I knew from Doris that Ernest had this money on him but my reliable little Doris had told no one else. And even if she had, even if it was known that he had money, nothing had been said at the Inquest about it. The only person at all likely to know that it had been taken was the man who took it. Yet 'Ernest was probably robbed of a good sum' Bertrand told me. He was annoyed, I think, that the theft had not been discovered. He had never thought (and who would?) of the pocket-case remaining in Ernest's hip pocket, which had convinced the police that Ernest had not been robbed. 'Find out what he had on him that night', he suggested, 'surely you or the police can do that'. Having removed and probably destroyed Ernest's roll he was peeved to find that this providing of a false motive had gone for nothing."

"That seems highly conjectural," said Mr Gorringer.

"I've told you, the whole thing is. But that wasn't my only reason for thinking that Bertrand robbed the corpse to suggest robbery as a motive. Ernest's money was from Emma and remained in an envelope 'with writing on it' as Doris said. When I asked Emma Rafter whether the family knew, *after* the murder, that she had been secretly in touch with her brother, she said, 'I think they guessed it. Or rather Bertrand did'. And when I asked her whether she eventually told the family she had sent money to Ernest she said, 'Bertrand seemed to know'. How could he have 'guessed' or 'seemed to know' if he had not seen that envelope addressed in her hand?

"Also he lied. He said distinctly that he was 'in the house alone from tea-time onward'. 'Fortunately I did not go out at all that evening'. Yet when Ernest phoned him there was no reply. Ernest told Mrs Locksley Rafter he had tried 'the others' but there was no reply. He also told Doris when she asked him. 'No. No reply from any of them', he said."

"Again, highly conjectural," said Mr Gorringer. "Ernest Rafter may not have tried his brother's number."

"Why not? It was in the book with the rest of them."

"Or he may actually have spoken to Colonel Rafter."

"If he did, Bertrand's lies are manifold. He said he was not even aware that Ernest had survived Burma until after the murder and in that I believe him. However, I'm not trying to prove my case. I'm admitting that it never could have been proved on the evidence in the first murder."

"You are not seriously suggesting, my good Deene, that Colonel Rafter not only disposed of his brother but subsequently chose to murder the wife of a local newsagent by the same repulsive method?"

"Of course. What else could he do? His original scheme had broken down. He had planned to kill someone without a motive, believing that he would thus be free of discovery, and by the worst possible bad luck he had chanced on his own brother, providing himself with a motive against all his intentions. He knew, both from their questioning of him and from me, that the police had each member of the family on their list of suspects. Above all, he knew from me that the Bullamys had seen him crossing the road that evening and believed they would know him again. That wouldn't have mattered if the murder had been of a stranger but, since it was of someone connected with himself and he was already something of a suspect, he felt his position becoming precarious.

"There was only one thing to be done—another murder for which he could not conceivably have a motive and for which Lobbin, already, as Bertrand knew from me, suspected of the first murder, would have a very strong motive.

"Let's suppose all this and watch Bertrand's movements from the start. He is, we will agree, a psychopath with a very conventional external character and appearance. He realizes the value of this in the circumstances. He decides on his crime and its venue. He does not go too often to the promenade at night but 'sometimes', as he told me. He had decided to wait for an occasion on which the promenade has few visitors and one of them is alone in the last shelter. He does not need an occasion on which Molly is away, but when she does go up to town for the night, he probably thinks it's a specially auspicious occasion and perhaps spends longer than usual down there waiting for his chance, so that there is no reply from his telephone when Ernest Rafter rings at about 7.15.

"He has provided himself with the weapon. Where this came from we may never know, but it certainly was not in ordinary use in his house, for he has no coal and the only hammer there is a lighter one kept in the tool chest. I daresay he had the idea of murder in his mind for years and kept this hammer concealed somewhere, perhaps since he moved to the town from some coal-heated home. At all events it was a weapon through which he could not be traced.

"He found what he had awaited for a long time, a man, probably half-drunk, huddled in a corner of the last shelter. He did his job and began walking smartly away. Having earlier joined the promenade at the point nearest to Marine Square, that is where the road forked away from the tarmac, he had met no one on his way to the shelter and expected to meet no one as he returned. But as he was approaching the fork, the first point at which he could leave the promenade, he saw coming towards him a man and woman whom he did not recognize—Mr and Mrs Bullamy taking their (still somewhat inexplicable) evening stroll.

"This did not alarm him in the least. But since they appeared to be strangers who would not in any case recognize him it would be better, he thought, to leave the promenade at the fork and cross the road so that he would not pass them. In this he rather misjudged the distance—or the striding power of the mannish Mrs Bullamy—for they were uncomfortably close to him before he could wheel left and he had to hurry to avoid coming face to face with them.

"However, all had gone as he anticipated and he could

186

congratulate himself when he reached his house, un-
noticed so far as he knew or we know. The couple he had
passed could not be sure of recognizing him again and
even if they were able to, what possible connection could
there be between Lieutenant-Colonel Rafter and the
murder of some wretched unknown man in a shelter?

"Imagine his feelings when he learned who that unknown man was. The very structure of his plan was
knocked away, for as everyone quickly knew he had a
motive for killing Ernest. Perhaps he had congratulated
himself, when he formulated his plan, on having found
one which no coincidence or bad luck could possibly
disturb, perhaps he realized now that there can be no
such plan. Coincidence, bad luck, destiny, or if you like
the Will of God cannot be flouted by even the cleverest
schemer.

"I think at first he almost expected the police to arrive
to arrest him. But as time passed and he was asked only
a few almost formal questions about his whereabouts and
he realized that there were other suspects—one far more
likely than himself—he grew easier. He had taken the
precaution of robbing the corpse and destroying the notes
he found and stressed robbery as a possible motive when
he discussed the matter with me. He was settling down
to wait for the arrest of Lobbin or for the whole thing
to be forgotten when on Christmas day I told him my
theory and said that the Bullamys would recognize the
road-crosser. That really frightened him, and he decided
to make sure Lobbin took the blame.

"He had, as I knew, been several times to Lobbin's
shop and seen the coal-hammer there. 'Bertrand's only
taken to coming to the shop lately' Lobbin told me.
Bertrand also knew that Lobbin was in the bar of the
Queen Victoria every evening from six to ten, because he
told me so. Finally, Bertrand had a very good reason to
get himself admitted by Mrs Lobbin. He only had to
say he wished to apologize for Mrs Dalbinney, or something of the sort, to settle the quarrel between Mrs Dalbinney and Mrs Lobbin, in fact, to be admitted by Bella.

"He had, as I knew, a hammer in his house and took this in the pocket of his overcoat. This second murder was forced on him by circumstances and fear and he had not time for the detailed planning he had done for the first. But he saw *how* to go about it. He would murder the woman with his own hammer then go downstairs to the shop for hers, blood it and leave it by her. It would be the means of hanging Lobbin. Meanwhile he would go home, scrupulously clean his own hammer and return it to the tool chest.

"All this he carried out with skill and good fortune. He was becoming an accomplished murderer now. He did not know that Mrs Cocking had watched his entry but in any case she could not see much of his face. Then he hurried home to arrange matters so that should anyone call, or should Molly French return, no one could guess that he had been out.

"I found him so 'settled' and established by his electric fireside that my respect for him as a clever murderer was lessened. He had overdone it. The smoking jacket and slippers, the calf-bound volume of Gibbon, the brandy and the nearly smoked cigar were a little too much, particularly since (as I discovered later) he had arranged to call for Molly French at that time. But what really gave him away was a piece of that petty parsimony for which he was known. He had not found it difficult to burn the paper money found on Ernest, but when he wanted to be discovered smoking the last of a cigar, he could not bring himself to throw away the length of Corona from which it had been cut and it was this I found in the box. He covered this as best he could. 'Not that. It's only half a cigar', he said jovially. But trivial as it may appear it provided me with one of the few pieces of evidence concrete enough to convince me."

"You think he anticipated your visit?" said Moore.

"Some visit, anyway. Mine or Molly's. When I reached Prince Albert Mansions Paul's first words to me were 'we rather wondered if you would come round'. They had

188

heard from the hall porter who was the husband of one of the barmaids at the Queen Victoria that the murder had happened. They may have phoned Bertrand. Or he may have sensed that I had my suspicions. At all events there was a big act intended to show that he had not been out that evening.

"His plan nearly came off, for I take it you would have charged Lobbin this evening at any rate with the second murder. I am the first to admit that though *all* the evidence I know of in this case is circumstantial there is at this moment *far* more of it against Lobbin than against Bertrand. I do not think Lobbin would have been convicted but I do think it is more likely, as matters stand, than the conviction of Bertrand. Further I think that it was because I have a touch of Bertrand's madness that I have been able to follow the ghastly distortions of his mind."

"You alarm me, Deene," said Mr Gorringer.

"There is no need for alarm, headmaster. I don't mean that I have any secret desire to kill. I mean that the lunatic, the murderer and the detective who has my kind of imagination, are all touched with the same frenzy. I could put myself in his place and follow his mad logic. It was only by doing so that I could identify him."

"To say that you have identified him is ludicrous," said Mr Gorringer. "You have produced nothing but your morbid imaginings to make us believe this story, which smacks more of the writings of Edgar Allan Poe than of real life. Has he, Inspector?"

"Nothing," said Moore.

"You see, Deene? You have failed to convince the Inspector, and you have made me rather indignant. I cannot see that you have produced for this theory of yours anything to which a judge or jury would listen."

"He hasn't," said Moore. "Yet I shall have to investigate it."

Mr Gorringer bridled.

"You will? It would seem, if I may say so, that you

would be guilty of dangerous blundering. Mrs Dalbinney has a number of highly influential friends who would not relish the involvement of her brother in such a cock-and-bull story."

Carolus, looking very tired, said, "I warned you, John, that I had almost nothing cogent to offer. The headmaster is quite right to say that no judge or jury would listen to it. But now it's up to you. It should not take you long to test it."

"It won't."

"There is first of all the chance of identification by the Bullamys or Mrs Cocking, or both. Then there is the hammer. You will find it in the tool chest in a small room at the back of the house. It will have been carefully cleaned but the microscope will pick out some traces of blood. Then someone must have seen Bertrand last night in the region of the Queen Victoria. But above all, there are his clothes. It is impossible that these murders could have been carried out by the method chosen without *some* blood getting on the murderer's overcoat. There may have been time to have the one worn for the first murder cleaned. But not for the second. You know what happens when someone tries to clean bloodstains out of cloth? Some trace is always left. Bertrand has no means of destroying the coat in the house, because Molly French is there, and if he dumped it somewhere you will know in time."

Moore smiled.

"I think you can leave all that to us, Carolus. It is rather more in our line than having the touch of madness which, you say, has enabled you to produce this theory."

"I reject the word 'theory'," pronounced Mr Gorringer.

"It is what I looked for from you, Carolus," Moore said. "The kind of wild hypothetical imaginary stuff which might easily turn out to hold the seeds of truth. But it is only when we get to work on it that it begins to make sense or otherwise. You wouldn't be much good without us back-room boys," said Moore good-naturedly, adding—" Let's have another drink."

It was eighteen months before Carolus had occasion to re-visit Selby-on-Sea and he found it basking in warm June sunlight. He drove along the road by the prom-enade, but could not see the last shelter from his car. When he reached the Queen Victoria, however, he found Doris and Vivienne still behind its bar.

" Well! " said Doris at once. " Fancy seeing you! It does seem a long time since you were here. I thought we might have heard something of you, but not a word. You're looking very well, isn't he, Vivienne? "

" Mmmm," said Vivienne in almost enthusiastic agree-ment.

Carolus invited them to have a drink. Vivienne said she didn't mind, and Doris said it was very kind of him.

" It was a shame about those murders," said Doris presently, " after all the work you did, too, for the police to get the credit. I don't suppose you minded, but I said to Vivienne, I wouldn't mind betting it was Mr Deene put them up to it, didn't I, Vivienne? Still they got him in the end, that's one thing. All those bloodstains on his coat—what else could they have been? Mr and Mrs Bul-lamy had to go over to Bawdon to give evidence at the trial, you know. They'd seen him crossing the road just after he'd done for this fellow with the staring eyes. They both picked him out separately on the identification parades. And that Mrs Cocking! She picked him, too, but you ought to have heard what she said about the police! She called them all the things she could lay her tongue to. But I expect you read about in the papers? "

" Yes," said Carolus.

" Of course he confessed in the end. Seemed quite proud of it, didn't he? Well, he wasn't in his right mind and that's a certainty. How he came to be a Colonel beats me. Fancy killing anyone like that! It gives you the creeps, doesn't it? "

" No," said Carolus, but smiled.

"All the family moved away from here afterwards. It was that Emma Rafter I was sorry for. I did hear they'd gone abroad and changed their name. Well, you can understand it, having two brothers like that. Mr Lobbin's still here, though. He's married again."

"Really?"

"Yes. A very nice party she is. Older than him, but seems to understand him more. He's started writing little bits in the paper. He was always clever. He's in here most nights, if you want to see him. He soon seemed to get over it, once they knew it wasn't him."

Doris served another customer but returned to give Carolus more news.

"That young policeman still comes in. Very pleased with himself, seems to be. I don't know why, because he's still in uniform, though; he hoped to go on the detective side. He married that young woman that was always about with him. So that's two weddings we've had."

"What about yours, Doris?"

"Mine? I like that! As if I should get married! I've got enough to think about as it is. Well, all I can say is, I hope we don't get another business like the one you were here for. Murders, and that. We don't want any more, thank you very much. We can do without that. Can't we, Vivienne?"

"Mmmm," agreed Vivienne, and raising her glass she faintly smiled.